"Do you want to hold him?"

Connor stretched out his arms and leaned toward Gage.

Gage scooted his chair back. "I'll try."

Connor babbled an unintelligible sound and kicked one leg against Skye's hip while leaning farther out of her grasp. He wasn't old enough to use words yet, but she understood his body language. She gently passed him to Gage.

Skye avoided eye contact and moved past him to the kitchen, wishing there was a wall or a cabinet or anything to block her view of Gage, cautiously holding Connor like he was the most fragile thing in the world. A telltale flutter in her midsection made her deliberately turn away and take her sweet time rummaging in the pantry for a container of the puffed rice snacks Connor loved.

That was the last thing she needed—succumbing to the image of this strong, competent man riding in like some fairy-tale hero to rescue the damsel in distress.

She wasn't in distress. Okay, maybe she had a little bit going on in her life, but she didn't need him to rescue her.

Heidi McCahan is a Pacific Northwest girl at heart, but now resides in North Carolina with her husband and three boys. When she isn't writing inspirational romance novels, Heidi can usually be found reading a book, enjoying a cup of coffee and avoiding the laundry pile. She's also a huge fan of dark chocolate and her adorable goldendoodle, Finn. She enjoys connecting with readers, so please visit her website, heidimccahan.com.

Books by Heidi McCahan

Love Inspired

The Firefighter's Twins
Their Baby Blessing

Their Baby Blessing

Heidi McCahan

Recycling programs
for this product may
not exist in your area.

LOVE INSPIRED BOOKS

ISBN-13: 978-1-335-47924-2

Their Baby Blessing

Copyright © 2019 by Heidi Blankenship

www.Harlequin.com

Printed in U.S.A.

Commit thy works unto the Lord,
and thy thoughts shall be established.
—*Proverbs* 16:3

To my Colorado family:
although we don't see each other often,
I'm thankful for the moments when
our paths intersect. Much love to all of you.

Chapter One

She shouldn't have said yes.

Seated at a table next to the window, Skye Tomlinson cupped both hands around her disposable coffee cup and scanned the parking lot outside Common Grounds for a man who might be Gage Westbrook. What was she thinking—meeting a total stranger for coffee? And after only a brief exchange of direct messages on social media, too. What if he'd fabricated his whole story? Maybe this was an elaborate scheme he'd plotted to—

Relax. Not every man was out to manipulate women for their own personal gain.

Skye took a sip of her skinny hazelnut latte, desperate for comfort as the painful memories of her ex-boyfriend threatened to resurface. He'd controlled her, mocking her need for independence. Then made her feel like nothing. Over and over. While his harsh words no longer played on an endless loop in her head, she still carefully guarded tender emotional wounds. And loathed her own foolishness at ever believing he genuinely loved her.

Stop. You're safe here. A quick glance around the newest coffee shop in Merritt's Crossing revealed two of her mother's friends sitting in the overstuffed chairs by the fireplace. More familiar faces lingered around tables, savoring the warm and inviting atmosphere on a blustery Sunday afternoon. She was confident any of these folks would come to her aid if she needed them.

Although she'd snooped around Gage's social media profile—or tried to anyway—he hadn't made many details available to her prying eyes. His profile picture featured a submarine, and his cover photo was a sunset over the Florida coast. On the upside, she'd asked her brother who worked at the local sheriff's department to run a quick check, and he'd come back squeaky-clean.

Despite Gage's spotless record, she was still apprehensive about meeting him. But he said he knew about baby Connor, and that he had sensitive information about the birth father. Maybe that meant he also knew more details about where Skye's cousin McKenna might be, so Skye couldn't afford not to hear what he had to say. Because as much as she adored the sweet eleven-month-old who'd been left in her care more than a month ago, it was time for McKenna to come back, step up and be Connor's mom.

While Skye hated the convoluted family feud that no doubt influenced her cousin's dangerous and heartbreaking life choices—and wrestled with her own guilt over not doing enough to help resolve it—she couldn't be Connor's permanent legal guardian. If she was honest, she didn't *want* to be his guardian. A temporary leave from her pharmaceutical sales position in Denver to come home to Merritt's Crossing and help her widowed mother while she recovered from knee surgery was manageable. Keeping the family furniture store afloat proved daunting, but Skye could handle it until Mom was back on her feet. Literally.

But motherhood? Though a noble endeavor, it wasn't part of her carefully orchestrated plans. Kids were fine for her friends, and she'd love it if her brothers married and started families someday, but she wasn't interested in raising Connor or having children. It wasn't just the day-to-day tasks of meeting Connor's needs and finding adequate child care, although juggling both responsibilities felt overwhelming. Caring for him threatened the self-reliance she'd worked so hard to gain. What was worse, with each passing day, Skye worried more and more that McKenna might not ever show up. The thought of parenting Connor on her own and managing a career planted an icy ball of dread in her stomach. She couldn't stand the thought of the precious baby boy going to foster care, though.

Common Grounds's front door opened, and a blast of frigid air accompanied a tall, broad-shouldered man wearing a dark green winter jacket and black knit hat. Her breath caught. Was that Gage? Although he'd worn exactly what he'd promised in his message so she could easily identify him, she wasn't prepared for his impressive physical appearance. The words *devastatingly handsome* darted through her mind.

Flustered by her reaction to his arrival, she willed the butterflies flitting through her abdomen to settle down while she let her eyes travel—just for a second—from his angular, clean-shaven jaw to his dark-washed jeans and what appeared to be new hiking boots. Interesting choice for a Colorado winter. Maybe he wasn't from around here?

The pleasant hum of conversation faltered as he removed his hat and surveyed the coffee shop. When his gaze landed on Skye and he strode toward her table, she felt the weight of every curious stare in the room.

She squirmed, pressing her spine against the rungs of her ladder-back chair, while her legs itched to stand and carry her to the safety of her car outside. If she was quick, she could brush past him. Offer a hasty excuse and cancel their meeting.

He stopped beside her, his fingers twisting his hat in his hands. She forced herself to meet his gaze. The flicker of uncertainty in his hazel eyes gave her pause. Was he nervous?

"Skye?"

She managed to find her voice. "Yes?"

"Gage Westbrook."

Skye clasped his outstretched hand, groaning inwardly as she realized the contrast between his cool skin and her clammy palm. "Nice to meet you," she mumbled and quickly pulled her hand away.

"It's nice to meet you, too." He gestured toward the counter behind him. "Mind if I grab a cup of coffee?"

His smooth voice and impeccable manners—not to mention those captivating eyes flecked with hints of gold—derailed her intentions. Any thought of getting up and leaving had vanished.

"Skye?"

Warmth heated her skin. "No, I—I don't mind. The coffee here's great."

"I'll be right back."

While Mr. Handsome-Hazel-Eyes strode to the counter, Skye avoided eye contact with anyone else in the room and pulled her phone from her purse. Her brother Drew had agreed to stay with Connor this afternoon while she met with Gage, and Mom went to church and then to lunch with a friend. Although Drew said he was willing to help, his lack of experience with babies put her on edge. Connor wasn't easy to care for. Would Drew be able to handle him?

Sure enough, two text messages waited for her. The first asking if they were out of diapers, and the second requested tips for coping with a fussy baby who refused to nap. She winced. Poor Drew. He wouldn't volunteer the next time she needed help. She sent a quick response and then set her phone down in front of her so she wouldn't miss another text.

A few minutes later, Gage slid into the seat across from her and set a steaming mug of black coffee on the table. He unzipped his jacket and draped it across the empty chair beside him. His aqua-blue sweater emphasized his muscular arms and shoulders, and Skye forced herself to avert her gaze. Gage settled in his chair and quickly smoothed his hand through his close-cropped sandy-blond hair.

"Thank you for meeting with me." His smile revealed straight white teeth and Skye's heart blipped double time. "I'm sure my message seemed odd."

Skye cradled her coffee again and strong-armed her thoughts into submission. Handsome or not, Gage was still a stranger, and she was only meeting with him to see if he could help her get what she wanted—a permanent guardian for Connor. "You said you found me because my cousin McKenna Tomlinson posted a picture online of the two of us at Christmas with her baby, Connor. It's unnerving, although not surprising, since she posted a lot of photos that day. The part I can't figure out is your connection to McKenna. I'd ask her myself, but she left town right after the holidays."

"I was afraid that might be the case." Gage frowned. "Do you know where she went?"

"Hard to say. She's…complicated. Last text I received

said she'd made some friends in Wichita." Skye picked at the cardboard sleeve on her cup. "I was hoping she'd reconnect with her mom, who lives in Kansas City now, but there's really no way to predict what McKenna might do next."

Not that McKenna's mother would bother to call if McKenna showed up in Kansas City anyway. Aunt Willa stopped speaking to Skye and the rest of their extended family a long time ago. The familiar regret over their long-standing feud made Skye's heart ache.

"And her baby?"

Gage's question pulled her back to the present. Her scalp prickled with uncertainty. "Before I say more about Connor, I'd like to know why you're asking. Who are you?"

"McKenna's boyfriend, Ryan, is—was—my best friend." Gage reached inside his jacket pocket and then slid a photograph across the table. "We were stationed in San Diego with the navy, and that's where he met McKenna."

"Oh." Skye examined the picture of Gage and a blond-haired, blue-eyed man standing on the beach, wearing shorts and T-shirts and grinning at the camera, with the ocean in the background. Ryan. Skye didn't know much about the guy with Gage, other than McKenna claimed he was Connor's father. McKenna's stories had always seemed a bit convoluted, though. It was reassuring to meet someone who could fill in some of the gaps, especially anything about Connor's father.

"I'm not sure what happened after San Diego," Gage said. "Ryan couldn't stop talking about her, but then we got our orders to transfer to Florida and he asked her to move there."

"She didn't, did she?"

Gage shook his head. "Ryan said he talked to her all the time and tried to convince her to change her mind, even offered her money to help cover the expenses. Then she told him she was pregnant, and he…" Gage looked away, and a muscle in his jaw knotted.

"He what?"

Gage dragged his gaze to meet hers. "He died before he could see her again or meet Connor."

"Oh no." Skye's stomach plummeted. "I'm so sorry. I—I had no idea. She never told me that part." No wonder Connor's father hadn't come forward to help. Questions pinged in her brain, and she wanted to ask more, but the sheen in Gage's eyes made her keep quiet.

"When did she come back to Merritt's Crossing?" His voice was shaky as he tucked the photo away.

"First she showed up at my apartment in Denver right before Thanksgiving, with Connor in his car seat, a backpack and five dollars to her name." Skye shivered at the memory. "I still don't know how she got to Denver from California with a newborn. Frankly, I was afraid to ask."

"So she and Connor lived with you?"

"I let them stay with me for a couple of days because I knew she didn't have anywhere else to go. We'd both lost so much, and it was nice to have family around, you know?" She clamped her mouth closed before she revealed details about her family's struggles. What was it about him that made her want to share information so freely?

"Where is Connor now?"

"My mom let McKenna and Connor move in with her in November. He's been staying with my mother and me since McKenna left in January, although my mom is recovering from knee-replacement surgery, and I'm trying to keep the furniture store open…" She trailed off. Again with too much information. *Stop.*

Gage studied her. "Sounds like a lot for one person to handle."

"I've managed so far, although it's been really hectic. As long as Connor doesn't get kicked out of the church's child care program, then it's all good." And given the program director's recent warning about Connor's behavior, that was definitely a possibility. She forced a wobbly smile. "I hope."

"Here's the thing. I made a promise to Ryan before he died." He worked his jaw before continuing.

A niggling in Skye's chest forced her to stiffen. "What kind of promise?"

"I told Ryan that I'd take care of his child, and I intend to keep my word."

What did he mean—*take care of his child*? She clenched her fists in her lap. "I don't understand. What are you—"

He held up his palm to silence her. "This sounds ridiculous, I'm sure, and I don't blame you for being skeptical, but—"

"*Skeptical* doesn't even begin to describe how I'm feeling." Skye linked her arms across her chest. "Why would I believe anything you tell me?"

Irritation flashed in his eyes. "Because Ryan was like a brother to me. I can assure you he had every intention of being involved in Connor's life."

Skye's throat tightened at the raw emotion in his voice.

"I—I want to do for Connor what Ryan can't." He cleared his throat. "I'd like to see him on a regular basis."

This was crazy. She didn't know this man, and he

wasn't even related to Connor. Did she really look that gullible? "I'm afraid that's out of the question."

Gage was not giving up. He'd come so close to finding Connor, only to encounter an unexpected obstacle—Skye Tomlinson. She was not only determined, but incredibly attractive. Her pink cheeks, long dark curls and pale blue eyes fringed with dark lashes all conspired against him and threatened to distract him from his critical mission. *Focus.*

He couldn't afford to blow his one chance and based on the way she was glaring at him, he estimated she was about three seconds from getting up and leaving.

"I'm sorry I've upset you." He softened his tone. "Is there anything I can say to change your mind?"

Something unreadable flickered in her gaze and vanished.

"Why are you here? I—I heard what you said about the promise to your friend, but do you really expect me to believe that you came all the way from Florida to find the baby he'd never met?"

The doubt in her voice pricked at him. What was wrong with a man keeping his word? Gage sipped his coffee and weighed his response. To be perfectly honest, he'd do anything to assuage the guilt he carried from watching helplessly while Ryan succumbed to the flames, knowing he could've saved him if only he'd followed the correct protocol.

No. Not now. He squeezed his eyes shut and battled back the mental images from that horrific day. Tomorrow was the one-year anniversary of the accident that killed his best friend, and he still had nightmares.

Setting his mug down, he met Skye's gaze again. "After eight years in the navy, I decided to not reenlist.

I'm almost finished with my online certification to become a wind energy technician, and the program's director told me he places most new graduates with companies in eastern Colorado or Wyoming."

"Ah." Skye nodded. "Alta Vista Energy just opened a new wind farm not far from here."

"I start my on-the-job training with them on Friday."

"Did you move to Merritt's Crossing hoping you'd find McKenna? Seems like a huge risk."

"I moved here because it offers the best chance at starting my second career, and the only time McKenna and I communicated, she mentioned she was trying to move back home. While your cousin sounds unpredictable, she shared a lot on social media up until a couple months ago. All of her recent posts were from this part of Colorado, so I assumed this was home."

Skye's gaze narrowed. "When did you talk to McKenna?"

"Just after Ryan's funeral. She wasn't there, and I was worried, so I sent her a text."

"But you've never heard from her again?"

"No." Gage leaned back in his chair. "She's ignored all my messages. I started looking for her as soon as I moved here, though. My first stop was a diner on the interstate near Limon because McKenna had posted that she worked there."

Skye scrunched up her nose in a way Gage found incredibly adorable. "Yeah, that job didn't last long. McKenna's not meant to be a waitress."

"That's what the owner told me. She also mentioned your family's furniture business here, and that someone might have more info if I stopped by the store. Honestly, I thought it was better to reach out online first. In case you didn't—"

Skye's phone buzzed on the table between them, interrupting his explanation. Her gaze toggled between him and the phone.

"Do you want to get that?" he asked.

"It's just a text. I'll read it later."

Six more notifications chimed in quick succession. He felt his mouth twitch but suppressed his smile. "Are you sure?"

"I'd better look. My babysitter is the only one who sends blasts of texts like that."

He waited while she studied the screen.

"Oh no." The appealing shade of pink on her cheeks faded to a pale white. "I can't believe this."

"Everything okay?"

She set the phone down. "Connor's babysitter just gave her notice. Her husband is being transferred to Phoenix, and she leaves on Saturday to look for a house there."

"I thought you said Connor was in day care at a church?"

Her hand trembled as she massaged her brow with well-manicured fingertips. "He is, but just two mornings a week because he's having issues."

"What kind of issues?"

"Biting." Skye heaved a sigh. "It's happened twice. Once more and they'll ask him to leave. That's why I hired a sitter for the other three days, hoping that if he wasn't around other kids quite so much, he'd get the one-on-one attention he seems to need."

"What will you do without a regular babysitter?"

"I—I don't know." She stared out the window.

A possible solution formed in his head. He hesitated. Given her earlier reaction, how would she respond if he mentioned he had a flexible afternoon schedule since most of his training could be completed in the mornings?

"I'm already on thin ice with the church's child care director. She thinks I shouldn't be Connor's guardian, that he'd be better off in a two-parent home. Anyway, if he bites another child again, I'm worried she'll use it as an excuse to call social services."

Not on his watch. Gage's heart fisted. "No." He wouldn't let that happen.

Skye flinched.

The single word came out more forceful than he'd intended. "I—I'm sorry." He held up both palms in surrender. "Please, don't let it come to that."

Skye's voice lowered to a whisper. "People talk. Look at how you found out about me from someone in Limon. Word will get out that I'm not able to care for him well enough and—"

"Skye." Gage's hand shot out and blanketed hers. "Let me help you. Please."

Her eyes widened, and she stiffened at his touch. Startled by the warmth that zinged up his arm, he scrambled to form a coherent thought. "I have afternoons free. Maybe some mornings, too. I can watch Connor as much or as little as you need."

The words tumbled out before he could stop them.

She stared at him. An awkward silence filled the space between them, and he suddenly regretted his bold offer. What if he scared her off?

Finally, the rumble of the espresso machine broke through the quiet, and she tugged her hand free. "I can't ask you to do that."

"You didn't ask. I offered."

She frowned. "Do you have any experience with babies?"

"I can learn." It was a weak argument. She'd probably say no for sure now. He held his breath. *Please say yes. Please say yes.*

"I—I don't know. I can't afford to risk Connor's safety with someone who lacks experience."

His gut cinched tighter and he leaned forward, fighting to keep his tone even. "And I can't go back on my word to my best friend. Give me two hours with Connor and let me prove to you that I can handle taking care of him."

She sighed and shrugged into her coat. "Come over for dinner tomorrow. I'll introduce you to my mother and Connor. We'll see how it goes."

Seriously? Relief washed over him. "What time?"

"Five thirty. I'll message you our address." She stood and reached for her purse. "See you then."

"Yeah. Great." His shock limited him to monosyllabic responses. "See you then," he called over his shoulder as her boots *click-click-clicked* across the hardwood floor behind him.

He'd done it. Somehow he'd convinced Skye to let him meet Connor. A smile tugged at his mouth and he pumped the air with his fist.

Through the window, he watched Skye jog toward her car as thick wet snowflakes fell from a gray sky. She was intense. And beautiful. He purged the observation from his thoughts. Nope. Not going there. He had one mission right now, and it didn't include flirting with a pretty brunette. Besides, he wasn't "relationship material." The last woman he'd dated in Florida had solidified that when she'd called him emotionally unavailable.

Gage gritted his teeth. He had his binge-drinking mother and absentee father to thank for that. And he knew firsthand how tough some foster homes could be. Maybe that was why he found Skye's loyalty to her own family both intriguing and intimidating.

He reached for his phone to check McKenna's social media for an update.

Still nothing. Gage sighed and revisited her older posts, landing on an image of McKenna holding Connor on her lap.

Man, Ryan would be so proud of his son. He hated that Ryan never had a chance to meet the baby before the accident.

"I'm going to look out for him. I won't let you down. I promise," Gage whispered, swallowing against the tightness in his throat. He didn't know yet how he would fulfill that promise specifically—looking out for an almost one-year-old—but it didn't lessen his resolve. He knew all too well the heartache of growing up without a dad, and he couldn't rest until he was certain Connor was safe. Loved. Being a part of Connor's life was about so much more than keeping a promise to Ryan. When Gage was a child, other adults had enabled his mother's reckless behavior. He never wanted Connor to experience the pain and hopelessness of that kind of betrayal from the very people who were supposed to protect him. And he'd do whatever it took to make that happen.

Chapter Two

She shouldn't have invited Gage over.

A dull ache throbbed at Skye's temples, and she'd snapped at Mom more than once this afternoon. The thought of allowing a man they'd just met into their home—into Connor's life—sent a shiver down her spine. She hurried to fix dinner in Mom's kitchen, while Connor sat at her feet, babbling as he pulled every single plastic container out of the bottom cabinet drawer.

Caught off guard by Gage's bold offer at the coffee shop yesterday, and still reeling from her babysitter's sudden resignation, she'd relented too easily. Her healthy suspicion of strangers had inconveniently vanished, and now, in less than ten minutes, he'd be at the door and she'd have to come up with a compelling reason why she didn't need his help. His desire to keep his promise to his friend was honorable and all, but she had to consider Connor's safety, too. What did she really know about Gage?

"There has to be another option," she muttered, sidestepping Connor to fish the salad-serving tongs out of the drawer.

"Honey, are you all right?" Mom sat at the oval table

in the breakfast nook, slicing tomatoes for the garden salad. "You've been talking to yourself all afternoon."

"Yep. Fine. I've just got a lot to think about." Skye skirted the L-shaped counter and set the tongs beside the salad bowl in front of Mom, then quickly pivoted away. She felt her mother's concerned gaze following her as she turned off the Crock-Pot. Gage and her child care issues paled in comparison to the furniture store's financial issues she'd stumbled across today. Dad had left a much more convoluted mess than Skye had originally thought. How in the world would she ever bring that up? Mom had endured so much already.

"That's a real shame about Bethany and her family moving to Phoenix," Mom said. "She was a wonderful babysitter."

"I wish she could've given more notice." Skye pulled a stack of plates from the cabinet and carried them to the table. "Her timing is the worst."

"Maybe God has something better in mind. For her and for you." Mom's gentle smile and trite observations made Skye bristle.

"You don't believe that's true."

"I didn't say that." Skye swiped her palm across her forehead and turned away to grab napkins and silverware. "It's just… Never mind."

Hurt filled Mom's brown eyes.

Skye clamped her mouth closed, conscious of poking holes in Mom's beliefs. Even though they were once her beliefs, too, she sure had a lot of doubts lately about what God must have in mind for her. For McKenna and Connor, too.

"I'm worried. I—I don't know what we're going to do without Bethany."

Without a lot of things. Skye kept her lengthy list of

worries to herself while she struggled to tamp down the anxious feelings twisting her up inside. If the business was in worse shape financially than she'd thought, and she had to hire a full-time babysitter for Connor while she tried to save the furniture store, her own personal savings account would dwindle quickly. Both of her brothers said they were committed to helping, but neither of them were prepared to financially support Mom, either.

"We've certainly endured quite a few surprises lately," Mom said quietly.

Connor squealed and banged two plastic measuring cups together, then held one out for her, accompanied by a toothy smile. Grateful his outburst might've saved her from discussing her waning faith, Skye leaned over and smoothed a wisp of his pale blond hair across his forehead.

"No, thanks. That's for you." When she pulled away without taking the measuring cup, his blue eyes filled with tears and his expression crumpled.

While his cries grew louder, Skye quickly glanced at the timer beside the oven. In two minutes, the rolls needed to come out. The stew in the Crock-Pot was ready, but there weren't drinks in the glasses yet, and she hadn't prepared anything for Connor to eat. Still so much to do before Gage arrived, and Mom wasn't mobile enough to carry hot dishes to the table. Letting him sit there and cry wasn't okay, either.

"C'mon, let's move to the living room and play with some trucks. Your favorite." She scooped him up and carried him into the living room, where his toys were still scattered across the beige carpet.

"Anything I can do?" Mom asked.

"I've got it." Skye set him on the floor and pushed

a plastic truck and some blocks toward him, but Connor only screamed louder, while his face deepened to a shade of pink she hadn't seen before in his previous tantrums.

"Wow." Skye glanced at Mom over her shoulder. "He's really angry."

"He'll calm down in a minute." Her mom braced against the table and pushed to a stand. "Let me—"

"No, don't get up." Skye hurried to her side and grasped her elbow. "I said I've got it. What do you need?"

"Honey, Dr. Bradley said I'm supposed to be walking short distances." Mom raised her voice to be heard above Connor's wailing. "There's no reason for me to sit here while you wear yourself out. I can at least carry a few things to the table."

Skye opened her mouth to argue, but the timer rang, reminding her that if she had any hope of getting the meal on the table, she'd have to relent and let her mother help a little bit.

"All right. I'll set the table while you get the rolls out of the oven."

"Deal." Mom patted Skye's arm and then moved slowly toward the kitchen.

"Oh, look at this." Skye brought Connor a bright-colored shape sorter from the toy bin beside the sofa, and thankfully he dialed back his cries to a pathetic whimper. While he examined the plastic shapes inside the rectangular box, Skye hurried to put plates and silverware on the table.

A few minutes later, the doorbell rang. *No.* A jolt of adrenaline zinged through her. She wasn't ready. She tucked a strand of hair that had escaped her ponytail behind her ear and glanced at her plaid button-down shirt and favorite skinny jeans. She'd meant to change before Gage—

Wait. Why did it matter how she looked? A relationship with him apart from their shared interest in Connor wasn't even on her radar.

She opened the door and Gage stood on the other side. His sandy-blond hair gleamed in the light from the porch, and the skin beside his hazel eyes crinkled when he smiled. A stunning smile that she was working hard not to stare at right now.

"Hey." That voice. Deep. Confident. Smooth. How could one simple word make her heart pound so easily?

Great. While most normal humans might return his casual greeting, Skye couldn't find her words. Or ignore Gage's shoulders, which seemed broader than she remembered. Or was it the green winter jacket that added bulk? Instead of speaking, all she could think about was how that shade of green emphasized the flecks in his eyes and—

"Skye?" Gage's brow arched. "You did say five thirty, didn't you?"

"Yeah, hi. Sorry, I was, uh…" *Just thinking about your amazing shoulders and gorgeous eyes.*

Oh brother. Warmth rushed to her face. "Please, come in."

She stepped back and pulled the door wide, while another wave of anxiety washed over her. Was she doing the right thing—allowing Gage to meet Connor? He'd been through so much in his first year of life. Introducing another stranger, even one with the best of intentions, made her uneasy.

The aroma of something delicious—soup, maybe—enveloped Gage as he toed off his boots inside the

Tomlinsons' front door. Definitely smelled more appealing than the canned chili he'd planned to fix for himself.

"Thanks for coming." Skye took his jacket, and his heart skittered at the way those pink lips of hers curved into a tentative smile.

He quickly banished those thoughts. "No problem."

"Hello, you must be Gage." A petite woman with salt-and-pepper curls and wearing black pants and a red blouse walked slowly from the kitchen to the nearby table, her eyes focused on a small basket balanced precariously in her hands.

"That's my mother, Rhonda Tomlinson," Skye said.

Before Gage could respond, Connor squealed so loud that Skye winced. "That's Connor's way of welcoming you."

Gage glanced at the little boy sitting in the middle of the living room floor, and his breath hitched. He'd recognize those blue eyes anywhere. They were a carbon copy of Ryan's. He swallowed hard and glanced at Skye again. "Mind if I say hello?"

"Please do." Something undecipherable flashed across Skye's features. "Dinner will be ready in a minute."

Gage approached slowly and sank onto the beige shag carpet. "What's up, little dude?"

Connor stared at him, wide-eyed, then babbled a string of unintelligible words while offering Gage an orange plastic dump truck.

"Thanks." Gage gently took the truck and drove it across the carpet and up Connor's leg, while making the appropriate truck noises.

Connor giggled and playfully pushed Gage's hand away.

Gage's heart expanded at the bubbly sound of Connor's

laugh, and he drove the truck along Connor's gray sweatpants again, making him laugh louder. This time Gage laughed right along with him, and they repeated the cycle. He quickly surveyed his surroundings—casual furnishings, floral curtains framing the windows, and shelves nearby lined with books and knickknacks indicated the Tomlinsons lived comfortably but didn't seem pretentious.

Feeling the weight of their stares, Gage glanced up to see Mrs. Tomlinson and Skye watching him, their mouths open.

Uh-oh. What had he done? "What's wrong?"

"Nothing's wrong. It's amazing." Skye's smooth brow furrowed. "We just haven't heard him laugh that much before."

Oh. Gage shifted his focus back to Connor. How sad. "He's got a great laugh. I'd want to hear more, too."

While Skye and her mother put dishes on the table, Connor offered Gage more of his toys, coupled with enthusiastic sounds, and Gage admired each car, plastic tool and rattle.

"I hate to interrupt the fun," Skye said, "but dinner is ready."

"All right." Gage stood, and Connor's lower lip wobbled.

Oh no. Gage hesitated. He'd made the kid cry already.

Connor's expression crumpled, and he stretched both arms toward Gage as if asking to be held. What should he do? He'd made his promise to Ryan without ever spending much time around children. Especially babies.

Gage shot Skye a panicked look.

Skye gave him a sympathetic smile. "That means he likes you and wants to keep playing. Why don't you sit down, and I'll put Connor in his high chair?"

So this crying was good? "Let's eat, bud." Gage angled his head toward the dining room table. Connor's response was a painful cry that knifed at Gage's heart. He groaned inwardly at his ignorant assumption that such a young child would make the transition to his high chair without complaint. Man, he had a lot to learn if he was going to make good on his commitment. What if Skye realized how inexperienced he was and refused to let him spend time with Connor?

Mrs. Tomlinson had already sat down. Gage waited until Skye had scooped Connor up and carried him to his high chair. The little boy arched his back and screeched, making it difficult for Skye to secure the harness and buckles.

"Wow." Gage grimaced. He might not be able to talk, but he'd made his preferences quite clear.

"He keeps us on our toes." Mrs. Tomlinson shook her head while Skye finally buckled Connor in and latched the white plastic tray in place. She straightened, her cheeks flushed, and claimed her place across from Gage.

"He'll calm down in a minute." Skye reached for her napkin. "Would you like to ask the blessing, Mom?"

Connor cried the whole time Mrs. Tomlinson prayed, drowning out most of what she said.

When she'd finished, Gage surveyed the meal. A basket of dinner rolls, green salad and a generous helping of beef stew in his bowl made his mouth water. He glanced at Connor. "Are you ready to eat?"

Connor paused his tirade long enough to consider Gage's question.

"Can he have some bread?" Gage asked Skye. He really had no idea what babies Connor's age could eat.

"Sure. If he throws it, he may not have any more,

though." Skye fired a warning glance in Connor's direction.

"Got it." No roll tossing at the table. Although it did sound a little fun.

Gage took a roll from the basket and pinched a small bite to share with Connor. "Here." He set it on the tray. "This bread looks yummy." His voice sounded goofy. And when was the last time he'd used the word *yummy*? He didn't dare look Skye's way.

Connor picked up the bread and popped it in his mouth.

Then his blue eyes widened, and he pointed toward the basket of rolls, while he bounced up and down against the high chair's vinyl cushion.

"Is it okay if he has more?" Gage asked.

Skye nodded, and he split another roll into chunks and handed it over. Connor gobbled it down as quickly as he could.

While Gage had anticipated the conversation might revolve around his reasons for moving to Merritt's Crossing, there wasn't much time to formulate a complete sentence. Once Connor realized Gage was willing to share from his plate, the little boy ate like he was a bottomless pit. Between putting food on the tray and trying to finish his own meal, dinner was almost over, and they hadn't had a chance to talk at all.

"You wouldn't know it by the way he's eating, but I promise we feed him on a regular basis. Or at least we try to." Mrs. Tomlinson scraped her own bowl clean. "Maybe you're our secret weapon, Gage."

"I don't know about that." Gage speared a bite of meat with his fork. "He's definitely got an appetite tonight."

A few minutes later, Connor shoved the chunks of carrots aside and rubbed his eyes with his fist.

"Yikes." Skye pushed back her chair. "I think he's about to melt down. Let me get him cleaned up before he rubs food in his hair."

"Is that usually what happens?" Gage asked.

"Sometimes." Mrs. Tomlinson chuckled. "We're not always great at figuring out when he's had enough."

Skye returned from the sink with a dishcloth in her hand. "I hadn't planned on giving him a bath tonight." She quickly wiped his fingers and his face while he did his best to squirm away.

Gage stifled a laugh. This kid had a strong will. Reminded him a lot of Ryan. The comparison felt like a gut punch, and his amusement vanished.

"Are you okay?" Mrs. Tomlinson reached over and patted Gage's arm. "You look sad all of a sudden."

How much to share? He'd already told Skye he wanted to be involved in Connor's life. Gage rubbed his fingertips along his jaw. "I hate that Ryan didn't get a chance to meet his son, you know?"

Mrs. Tomlinson's eyes filled with empathy. "We wish things were different, too. I'm sure Skye told you we don't know if McKenna will return. Maybe God brought you into our lives for a reason."

"Mom—" Skye shot her mother a warning glance.

"It's true, whether you choose to believe it or not." Mrs. Tomlinson frowned at her daughter. "We don't know if she'll come back. What if she doesn't? Gage's connection to Connor's father isn't a coincidence."

Skye lowered Connor to the floor. He quickly crawled across the carpet to the toys he'd played with before dinner.

Gage tried to assess Skye's reaction to her mother's feelings. She seemed like she had a lot going on in her life. He didn't dare ask, but did she really plan on caring for Connor on her own if his mother wasn't willing or able to care for him?

"Like I said yesterday, I'm finishing my certification through the wind energy technician program at the community college. I'll start the hands-on training soon, and until I'm placed in a full-time position, I have a flexible schedule."

"See?" Mrs. Tomlinson beamed at her daughter. "A flexible schedule. That's exactly what we need."

Skye sank into her chair. Uncertainty was written all over her face. She sighed. "Can you come over tomorrow afternoon? From three to five thirty?"

"Absolutely."

"Okay. I'll leave a list of instructions for you. Mom will be here, too, just in case."

Gage ducked his head and suppressed a smile. Her subtext was not lost on him. *Just in case you're a lousy babysitter.*

"Now that we have that worked out, how about dessert?" Mrs. Tomlinson asked.

"I think I'll pass." Gage pushed back his chair and stood. "I still have some unpacking to do, and a test to study for."

"Oh, I'm sorry to hear that." Mrs. Tomlinson frowned. "Would you like to take some brownies home? Or maybe the leftover stew?"

"No, thank you." He didn't want to overstay his welcome. Skye's body language indicated she wasn't thrilled about what just happened, and he wanted to go before she changed her mind about tomorrow. "It was delicious, though."

"I'll walk you out." Skye crossed to the front door, pausing to pick Connor up and wedge him on her hip. He immediately gave her a sleepy smile and grabbed a chunk of her ponytail in his chubby fist.

She gently extracted her hair from Connor's hand and pressed a gentle kiss to his forehead.

Gage looked away and jammed his feet into his boots. So she wasn't a total ice queen. Maybe she was too stressed and overwhelmed. Or just not a fan of him dropping into her life unannounced? She'd mentioned her concerns about someone calling social services. Did she think he was going to try to take Connor from her?

Something told him now was not the time to offer reassurances. He put on his jacket and paused, one hand on the doorknob, and dared to look at her one more time. "Thanks for giving me a chance."

"Don't let me down."

Wow. Okay. "See you soon."

"Good night."

He stepped out onto the porch and pulled the door closed behind him. Staring up into the night sky, his breath puffing in little white clouds, he silently offered a prayer for guidance.

I'm off to a shaky start here, Lord.

When he set out to find McKenna and her baby, he never anticipated meeting Skye. And no matter how hard he tried, he couldn't ignore his initial attraction to her. Not that it mattered. She was downright frigid tonight and clearly didn't like strangers, no matter how honorable their intentions. She'd probably only asked for his help because her mom coaxed her and she was desperate. But he couldn't let her attitude discourage him. He owed it to Ryan to keep his promise.

Chapter Three

Please, please let this be the one.

Skye folded her hands behind her back and pasted on a polite smile. Her customers, Mr. and Mrs. Crawford, circled the eight-piece dining room set in the furniture's showroom for the third time, their brows furrowed.

"What do you think, sweetheart?" Mr. Crawford clapped his hand on his wife's shoulder, while he jangled his loose change with his hand in his other pocket. Skye held her breath, waiting for Mrs. Crawford to answer.

"I just can't make up my mind. Do you think we can all fit around it for Easter? We're hosting this year."

Yes, of course. Skye dug her fingernails into her palm to keep from blurting out a response. She'd actually never visited the Crawfords' home and had no idea how much space they had in their dining room, but the store's dismal sales—almost nonexistent this month—could really use a boost.

"It might be a tight squeeze, especially with the credenza, too, but I'm sure we can make it work." Mr. Crawford gave Skye a reassuring smile, the lines on his weathered face crinkling around his eyes.

She widened her smile, while the tension between her shoulders knotted tighter. Mrs. Crawford did not seem convinced.

"We really love the bedroom set we purchased from your daddy some years ago," Mrs. Crawford said, running her hand over the oak tabletop. "Now that our son and his wife moved to Fort Collins and took our dining room table and chairs, I'd really like something that will accommodate him and his wife, and of course, any future grandchildren, if our daughter ever gets married…" She trailed off and stepped back as if to gain a better perspective.

"I'm glad you've enjoyed your bedroom set." Skye kept her tone warm. Optimistic. "We always appreciate loyal customers."

"Your father was a great guy." Mr. Crawford's gaze filled with empathy. "We had a good time coaching your brother's Little League team together all those years. How's your mom doing?"

Skye swallowed hard, surprised by the emotion unexpectedly rising at the mention of her father's good works in Merritt's Crossing. "Mom's getting by. I guess you heard she's had knee replacement surgery. The recovery's tougher than we expected."

"I can imagine." Mr. Crawford glanced at his wife, the change in his pocket jangling a little louder. "What do you say, hon? Is this the one or—"

Skye's phone rang, and she froze. Ignore it? What if it was McKenna? But taking the call meant stepping away from the customers, and she hated for them to think they weren't important. Quite the opposite, really.

"Go ahead and answer that if you need to, dear." Mrs. Crawford smiled politely. "We don't mind."

"I'll just be a minute." Skye crossed the showroom

in quick strides to the antique rolltop desk that served as the home base when she couldn't be in the tiny back office. Business cards, a work space for her laptop and a vase of pink carnations with a sprig of baby's breath decorated the well-worn surface. Her phone's screen lit up with the church's number in the caller ID. *Oh no.* Her stomach dropped. Connor.

"H-hello?" she said, unable to keep the tremor from her voice.

"Hello, Skye, this is Betty Sanders over at the church. How are you?"

Skye squeezed her eyes shut. A call from the child care director wasn't a good thing. "I'm fine, Mrs. Sanders. How can I help you?"

"We've run into a bit of an issue with Connor this morning. Do you have a few minutes to chat?"

Skye opened her eyes and glanced over her shoulder. Mr. and Mrs. Crawford stood close together near the dining room set, talking quietly. At least they hadn't left. Yet. "What happened?"

"I'm afraid he bit another child on the arm. As we've already discussed, biting is a cause for concern. Since it's happened two other times, we're going to have to ask you to leave the Mom's Morning Out program."

No, no, no. Skye pressed her hand to her cheek. "I'm sure you're aware Connor's had a lot to deal with lately, with his mom…out of town for a while. I mean, he's not even one yet. Isn't there a chance he's just trying to express his frustration—"

"Skye, we can't allow him to bite. It's not fair to the other children."

"But he isn't trying to be aggressive. He's never bitten me or my mom or anyone outside the nursery. How do you know he wasn't provoked?" She knew she was pushing her limit with Mrs. Sanders, but she couldn't help but try. The Mom's Morning Out program was her child care lifeline. Without it, she had nothing. Well, nothing except Gage.

"I can assure you he was not provoked," Mrs. Sanders said, her tone icy. "As the director, I have a responsibility to provide a safe and nurturing environment for all who attend. While it's a real shame about Connor's abandonment, I'm not going to excuse his unacceptable behavior."

Skye bristled at the older woman's harsh, judgmental tone. She bit her lip and glanced at her customers again.

Mr. and Mrs. Crawford were already halfway to the store's front door. "We'll be back," they whispered.

No! She wanted to run ahead and plant herself in their path, maybe even offer them a discount off the full price. At this point, she wasn't above begging them to reconsider. She really couldn't afford to lose this sale.

"Skye?" Mrs. Sanders's voice grated on her nerves. "Are you still there?"

"Yes, I just—"

"I'll need you to come pick Connor up immediately."

"What?" Skye glanced at the oversize wooden clock mounted on the wall, the hands on the distressed finish inching toward eleven o'clock. "I usually don't pick him up until twelve fifteen."

"Perhaps I wasn't explicit enough. He's being removed from the program. Permanently. I expect to see you here in the next fifteen minutes."

"But—"

There was no point arguing. Mrs. Sanders had already ended the call. Skye pulled the phone away from her ear and stared at it in disbelief. This couldn't be happening. What was she going to do with an eleven-month-old in a furniture store? Sure, she could set up the portable crib to keep him contained in the back room, but he wouldn't be content there for more than a few minutes. And he'd never take a nap there, either.

Oh, McKenna. What have you done?

With Connor's first birthday coming up in a few days, surely her cousin would come home in time to celebrate?

Tears stung her eyes, but Skye refused to fall apart right now. She didn't have time for a meltdown, and she wouldn't give Mrs. Sanders the satisfaction of seeing her cry. After hastily scrawling a note indicating the store's unexpected closure due to a family emergency, she taped it to the glass door on her way out. This was one more reason why sales had to improve—she needed the income to hire additional help.

Another storm had blown in, and fresh snow blanketed the sidewalk in front of the store. She made a mental note to ask Drew to stop by and shovel it after work. Again. Ducking her chin against the flakes swirling around her, Skye trudged to her car parked behind the store, the reality of her circumstances weighting her steps.

A mother who could barely walk, an abandoned baby without a babysitter and her family's floundering furniture business, not to mention zero resolutions within her grasp.

What about Gage?

She pushed out a laugh at the ridiculous notion. They barely knew anything about him, and he hadn't even spent a single minute alone with Connor. How could he possibly be the answer to her problems?

Gage eased his truck into the Tomlinsons' driveway and turned off the ignition, wishing he could do the same for the anxiety wreaking havoc on his insides. Man, he hadn't felt this nervous since his first week at sea on the submarine. Sure, he and Connor got along great last night, but they hadn't been alone. He'd only played with a couple of toys and shared some food at dinner. Skye did most of the work, and she'd intervened when Connor threw a fit.

What if he totally messed this up?

An ache formed in his chest. Yesterday marked one year since Ryan died. He glanced at the picture wedged on his dashboard, the one of him and Ryan on the beach in San Diego that he'd shared with Skye at the coffee shop. After their meeting, he'd tucked the dog-eared photo inside one of the few books he owned, but this morning he'd mustered the courage to retrieve the picture and tuck it into the corner of his dash—a frequent reminder spurring him on to keep his promise.

Pocketing his keys, he climbed out of the truck and slammed the door. Although the snow had stopped falling, several inches coated the driveway, a sedan parked in front of the garage and the steps leading up to the Tomlinsons' modest rambler. Should he offer to shovel while he was here? Or maybe Skye wanted to take care of that herself, too.

He climbed the steps and the door swung open before he could knock or ring the bell.

"Hey," Skye greeted him, looking as though she'd stepped out of a corporate boardroom in a long gray dress belted at the waist and stylish black boots. His gaze flitted from her hair piled in a messy bun on top of her head, to her red-rimmed eyes and blotchy cheeks. Had she been crying? His chest tightened. Did something happen to Connor?

"Are you all right?"

"Come on in." She stepped back, ignoring his question. "I didn't want you to ring the bell. Connor's still taking a nap."

Gage stood in the foyer and quickly surveyed his surroundings. The house was quiet, and he didn't want to do anything that might upset her more. He was also afraid to ask why she wasn't at the furniture store. Maybe she'd decided she didn't trust him being there without her supervision after all.

"My mom will be home from her physical therapy appointment soon." Skye crossed to the table in the breakfast nook, where a can of soda and a bag of chips sat between a laptop and a large calendar. Did she have another job she hadn't mentioned? He shifted from one foot to the other, and kept his coat and his boots on, worried that one wrong move might earn him an icy stare.

She slumped into the chair with a sigh, then shot him a look, her smooth brow furrowed. "Why are you just standing there?"

"I'm waiting for my orders."

"What?"

"My orders. You look stressed. Or busy. Maybe both. If you need to get some work done, I'd be glad to shovel the driveway or something until Connor wakes up."

"You don't work for me." She massaged her forehead with her fingertips. "I'm not going to ask you to shovel my driveway. Or boss you around."

Okay. He ducked his head to hide the smile tugging at the corners of his mouth. This was probably not the best time to mention that she'd been bossy since the first second they'd met. He took his time unlacing his boots and hanging his jacket on the rack near the door. How long did a baby sleep anyway? Hopefully not much longer. Gage needed Connor to wake up and save him from Skye and her fragile mood.

He padded in his socks toward the table and slowly eased into the chair across from her. He wasn't good with females and tears. No matter how hard he tried, he always seemed to say the wrong thing. Did she want to talk about it? She sure didn't seem like she wanted his help. While he racked his brain for something safe to say, her phone chimed, and she pounced on it. She swiped at the screen, her eyes quickly scanning, and then she flung the phone back on the table in disgust.

Oh boy. Gage wiped his sweaty palms on the legs of his jeans and braced for a fresh wave of tears.

"Perfect. Just perfect." She glared daggers at the phone and shook her head. "I can't believe this is happening."

"Do you want to talk about it?"

"Connor got kicked out of the church day care today."

Well. That explained a few things. "Why?"

"Bit another child. Third offense. They made me pick him up early." Her eyes brimmed with tears. "I don't know what I'm going to do," she whispered.

Please, please don't cry. Gage's knee bounced up and down under the table, and he scrambled for a pragmatic solution to get in front of her impending meltdown. "Can you appeal the decision?"

"Tried that. The senior pastor just texted me and said the director of the program has the final say." Skye reached for her phone again. "I really need to find someone who can watch Connor on a consistent basis. Most of the time he still takes two naps, so it's just a few hours each day—and only until Mom gets some of her mobility back. I've called everyone I can think of, though."

You haven't asked me. Gage clamped his mouth shut. What would she say if he offered?

She frowned, shaking her head as she scrolled some more. "Mom wants me to hire someone to manage the store so I can stay with Connor, but we just don't have any wiggle room in the budget…" She heaved another sigh. "And I don't have the heart to tell her about our financial situation right now, on top of everything else she's dealing with."

Her troubled gaze toggled to him. "Sorry to dump all this on you. Probably way more than you wanted to know."

Not true. He did want to know because he honestly wanted to help, and although the sheen of moisture in her beautiful blue eyes had subsided, he was going to tread lightly. She seemed guarded—suspicious, even— of his intentions. He really didn't want to blow his chance at being in Connor's life, or risk ignoring his pledge to Ryan. And what if word got out of Connor's situation and someone called social services?

Adrenaline slammed into him at the mental images that scenario conjured.

She narrowed her eyes. "What are you thinking?"

He shifted in his chair. *Here goes nothing.* "I—I know you're in a bind, and I totally get that you might have issues with accepting help from strangers—"

"I do not."

Really? Gage silently cocked an eyebrow.

She ducked her chin. "Okay, maybe a little."

"My schedule is flexible until I start the practical portion of my training, and I'd be glad to stay with Connor whenever you need me to."

She picked at her thumbnail and avoided his gaze. "I don't think that's a good idea."

"Why not?"

The sound of Connor crying came through the baby monitor resting on the kitchen counter nearby.

Lousy timing, kiddo. Gage studied her, hoping she wouldn't use that as an opportune time to escape the conversation.

"I'd better get him." Skye's phone chimed again, and she picked it up, glanced at the screen, then pushed to her feet and hurried down the hallway.

"Skye—"

She didn't turn back, and a minute later, he listened through the monitor as she spoke to Connor and his crying ceased.

Gage tipped his head back and stared at the ceiling. No, he didn't have any experience with babies. Or children at all, really. His brief stints in and out of temporary foster care placement had left a scar, though, and he couldn't fathom letting Connor grow up without consistent, stable male role models.

He smoothed his hand over his close-cropped hair and silently prayed for the words to change Skye's mind. Ryan was the closest thing to a brother he'd ever had and being a part of Connor's world was the only way Gage could express his gratitude for the bond they'd shared.

No, no, no. Skye's fingers trembled as she knelt on the floor beside Connor, trying to keep him from wiggling out of reach while she changed his diaper.

While Gage's story about his connection with Ryan seemed legitimate, and the photo he shared lined up with what little McKenna had shared about Connor's father, was Gage really the solution to her babysitting needs? What if she accepted his offer and he decided it wasn't for him? He said he was committed to being involved in Connor's life, but did he even know what that meant? She'd never forgive herself if Connor was hurt because she'd made a hasty decision. The wounds were still raw from the last time she'd allowed herself to be vulnerable. Suffering the consequences of her poor decisions was one thing, but what if her choices impacted an innocent child, too?

The thought made her stomach churn.

Out in the living room, she heard the front door open and Mom exchanging greetings with Gage. Connor's eyes followed her as she tossed the diaper in the trash. She pushed to her feet, eager to get back to the other room before Gage had a chance to woo her mother. Connor sucked loudly on his thumb while she lifted him off the floor. "Let's get a snack, sweet pea."

She strode down the hallway with Connor in her arms. Mom and Gage sat at the table, talking quietly. What had she missed? Fatigue lined Mom's face, and Skye cringed inwardly. Although she was probably trying to be a good sport and chat with Gage, Mom normally went straight to the couch and elevated her leg after physical therapy.

"Hi, Mom. How was your appointment?"

Mom gave her a tired smile and reached over to give Connor's leg a gentle squeeze. "It was all right. My therapist pushed me hard."

"Would you mind holding him while I fix his snack?" Skye hovered near Mom's shoulder. She hated to ask her to do anything extra, but maybe Connor wouldn't cry if he snuggled with Mom.

"For a minute." She stifled a yawn. "I'm fading fast. Might need a nap before dinner."

Connor stretched out his arms and leaned toward Gage.

"Do you want to hold him?" Skye couldn't keep the surprise from her voice.

Gage scooted his chair back. "I'll try."

Connor babbled an unintelligible sound and kicked one leg against Skye's hip, while leaning farther out of her grasp. He wasn't old enough to use words yet, but she understood his body language. She gently passed him to Gage, acutely aware of the warmth of Gage's fingers brushing against hers.

Skye avoided eye contact and moved past him to the kitchen, wishing there was a wall or a cabinet or anything to block her view of Gage, with his powder blue long-sleeve shirt hugging the defined curves of his muscular arms, cautiously holding Connor like he was the most fragile thing in the world. A telltale flutter in her midsection made her deliberately turn away and take her sweet time rummaging in the pantry for a container of the puffed-rice snacks Connor loved.

That was the last thing she needed—succumbing to the image of this strong, competent man riding in like some fairy-tale hero to rescue the damsel in distress.

She wasn't in distress. Okay, maybe she had a little bit going on in her life, but she didn't need him to rescue her.

"Gage was just telling me he might be the solution to your child care dilemma," Mom said, her tone hinting that she was completely on board with the idea.

The round metal container slipped from Skye's hands and rolled across the hardwood. Blood pounded in her ears as she chased after it. Gage was watching her—she could feel the weight of those gorgeous hazel eyes tracking her. Did he sense her apprehension?

She straightened, just in time to catch Connor looking up at Gage, his little hand exploring his face, and his pudgy cheeks scrunched in an adoring smile.

Oh brother. Don't tell me you're captivated, too.

"We didn't get a chance to discuss it."

Mom shot her a look. "What's to discuss? You need someone consistent and reliable, with flexibility in their schedule. And I'll be here to advise Gage on what to do."

But what about long-term? What kind of impact would Gage's role in Connor's life have? She bit her lip and stole another glance at Connor. He babbled and cooed, his fingers meandering around Gage's angular jaw. When Gage mimicked a playful bite toward Connor's hand, the little boy's belly laugh made Skye's breath catch.

Mom caught her staring and arched a brow as if to say, *See?*

Skye averted her gaze and poured the rice puffs into a small plastic bowl, then carried it to the table.

"I know you wanted Connor to spend time with other children, but given his history with biting, and as long as he's still taking two naps, maybe keeping him here is the best thing for now. Gage can come by for a few hours. Between the two of us, we—"

"All right." Exasperated, Skye cut her off. "Point taken."

Connor stopped jabbering and stared at her, his lower lip pooched out. Gage and Mom both glanced at her, eyes wide.

"I'm sorry." She softened her tone as she set the bowl on the table in front of Gage and Connor. "That sounded harsh."

An awkward silence blanketed them, and she returned to the kitchen to put some water in a sippy cup for Connor, her face flaming. Again. She only wanted to do what was best for Connor, but now she felt like the irrational one. How did that happen?

"I think what Skye is trying to convey is that we weren't really prepared for any of this," Mom said. "McKenna has always been wild and impulsive, but she didn't give us any indication that she planned to leave him. Once she settled in here, she seemed content. But now that she's gone, we want to make sure we do the right thing. Between caring for Connor, the store and my surgery… This is a lot for us to handle."

Skye felt the tension in her shoulders loosen. There. *Ditto*, she wanted to say, but that sounded ridiculously inadequate. Not to mention childish. Gage probably thought she was a mess.

"I totally get it." Gage's deep voice was filled with empathy. Compassion. "It's a radical idea, me coming here, claiming a connection to this child and offering to help. I don't blame you for being skeptical. I'm glad you're questioning my intentions."

This time it was Skye's turn to stare in disbelief. "You are?"

"Absolutely. You can't be too careful." Gage shifted Connor to the crook of his opposite arm. "Let me assure you, again, that I want what's best for my friend's son, too."

"Of course you do." Her mother reached over and patted his hand. "I'm going to leave you two to iron out the details. I'm beat."

While Mom stood and slowly worked her way down the hall toward her bedroom, Skye tried to offer Connor the sippy cup, but he pushed her hand away and reached for more of his snack. She sighed and left the cup on the table before circling around to her chair and the calendar she'd abandoned earlier. "Aunt Linda just texted me and said she'd help in a pinch, so I have the next few days covered. How soon can you start?"

"How about next week?"

She hesitated, then picked up her pencil. "Sure, next week is…fine. Is one to five in the afternoon okay?"

"Sounds great."

She wrote his name and the time on the calendar. "And how about after that?"

"How far out would you like to schedule?"

Her stomach churned as her pencil hovered over the calendar. Were they really doing this? Had she just agreed to let Gage watch Connor as often as he wanted? "H-how about Tuesday, Wednesday and Thursday afternoons from one to five for now?"

"Perfect." She heard the smile in his voice and dragged her gaze to meet his. She wasn't at all prepared for the gratitude she'd find in those gold-flecked eyes.

"Thank you for giving me a chance to honor my word." His voice was gritty, emotional this time. "I won't let you down."

"Good." Uncertainty still weighed heavily as she quickly looked away and wrote his name on the dates they'd agreed on. A chance to honor his word? Yes. Not a permanent place in their lives, though. Sure, he'd looked super attractive holding Connor safely in his arms, but clearly it had muddled her thinking. No matter how much Gage's attentiveness toward Connor tugged at her heartstrings, she had to maintain firm boundaries. Strong men like Gage only used their power to control women, and she wouldn't allow herself to fall for him.

Chapter Four

❧

Gage quickly anchored the metal carabiners of his harness straps to the safety rails along the platform's perimeter, then stood up. Cold air filled his lungs and he pivoted slowly, admiring the snow-covered wheat fields checkering the landscape in every direction. Despite the additional weight of his equipment, the view from the top of the wind turbine was worth the effort. A brilliant blue sky—a particular shade he'd heard was unique to Colorado—stretched overhead, and the late-afternoon sun made the moisture on the giant white blades glisten.

"Not a bad first climb, right?" Danc, one of his new partners for today's orientation, glanced back over his shoulder and grinned, arms stretched wide.

"Can't complain." Gage couldn't manage much more than a two-word reply. While he'd thought he'd maintained his physical fitness since he left the navy, his aching muscles protested from the three-hundred-foot climb. Clearly, he still had some work to do in the gym.

"Let's check on this beacon." Max, their team leader, summoned them to the red light nearby that was supposed to blink constantly, alerting approaching aircraft.

Gage complied, taking tentative steps toward Max.

He might've spent weeks at sea living in a submarine in the depths of the ocean, but wearing a harness tethered to a tower in the middle of miles of farmland made his mouth dry and legs jittery. The height didn't seem to be the problem. He'd always loved the advantage of seeing the world from this perspective. Maybe it was the apprehension of working with a partner again that had his insides twisted in knots. Squashing thoughts of Ryan, he slowed his breathing and followed Max's and Dane's instructions. At least they were working in a team of three. Safety in numbers, right?

"The first day's always a tough one. Relax." Max offered Gage a reassuring smile. "You'll get the hang of it."

"Hope so." Did his lack of confidence seem that obvious? He hadn't had any trouble with his online courses, and he'd assumed starting the hands-on training would be less demanding than anything he'd experienced in the military. But after spending several hours with Max and Dane examining the interior portions of the turbine, his head felt like it was going to explode. The biting wind buffeting them, combined with the odd sensation of his harness and straps shadowing his every move, brought a whole new meaning to the phrase *on-the-job training*.

"This is a straightforward repair." Dane handed Max the new lightbulb. "We'll have this changed out in no time."

Gage squatted beside them and focused on Max's careful instruction, trying to memorize all the details he and Dane noted. An hour later, they had the new bulb installed, the cover in place and their tools packed up.

"Let's go, boys. It's quitting time." Max led the way toward the hatch.

They unlatched from the rail, then lowered themselves through the narrow opening and reconnected their harnesses to the pulley system inside the tower. Dane started the descent first, followed by Gage, while Max went last to make sure the hatch was closed properly.

Gage's heavy boots squeaked on the rungs and sweat trickled along his spine as he climbed down the ladder. Why wasn't this easier than going up? Dane and Max bantered back and forth, their words echoing off the walls of the tower. Gage trained his gaze on the next rung and kept quiet.

A few blessed minutes later, his feet touched the solid concrete floor.

"Well done." Max clapped him on the shoulder. "Let's celebrate your first trip to the top with the boys over at Angie's. They've got a Friday night special that's hard to beat. What do you think?"

Gage hesitated.

"C'mon, man," Dane urged. "It's like a rite of passage for all the trainees."

Gage stepped out of his harness and stalled for more time to respond. He wasn't about to admit he was wiped out. After the stress of his full day of orientation and climbing the tower in the cold, all he wanted to do was sleep until noon tomorrow. Dane and Max seemed like the kind of guys who'd give him a hard time about that, though. Besides, he'd missed the camaraderie of hanging out with other men—the harmless teasing, casual conversation, the inside jokes that made him feel like part of a group.

"Yeah, that sounds good." He smiled, then quickly stowed his gear and climbed inside the company truck.

Max drove while Dane rode in the passenger seat, and Gage sat behind Dane in the truck's extended cab. They made small talk on the drive back to Alta Vista's offices, and Gage felt the tension in his weary shoulders slowly release. Warmth from the truck's heater chased away the bone-deep chill, too.

Once Max parked near the maintenance garage, they unloaded their gear and tools inside.

"You know the way to the diner?" Dane stopped inside the garage doorway, jangling his keys in his hand.

Gage nodded. "Across the street from the furniture store, right?"

Dane grinned. "That's the one. By the way, if you need anything for your new place, I highly recommend Tomlinson's." He released a long whistle. "Skye Tomlinson is running the place right now, and she is easy on the eyes. Know what I mean?"

Gage gritted his teeth. He knew exactly what he meant. "Thanks for the tip. See you in a few." He turned and strode toward his own truck. Dane's comment bothered him more than it should. He was right—Skye was a beautiful woman. Was it the tone that pricked at him? Or the knowledge that Dane had noticed and didn't mind sharing his observations?

He started the engine and followed Max's and Dane's vehicles out of the parking lot, his headlights bouncing across the snowbanks lining the road. A light snow started falling, and he turned on the wipers to clear his windshield.

Why did he care what Dane thought? Gage barely knew Skye. They were two adults forging a friendship and keeping Connor's best interests as their shared focus. It wasn't like he had any interest in dating her.

Did he?

* * *

Connor flung another french fry onto the floor of the diner and followed it up with a defiant glare.

Skye wanted to scream. Why had she agreed to bring Mom to her book club in Angie's meeting room? The outing had seemed simple at first, and her mom had looked forward to it all week. They hadn't considered how Connor might react, though.

"No throwing food, remember?" Skye tried to keep her voice even while she gave him her most pointed stare.

His lower lip pooched out, and he made a throwing motion even though his hand was empty.

What a stinker. She bit her lip and glanced away. Another family with three young children sat at a booth nearby. None of the kids were flinging their food on the floor. The adults looked like they were actually having a conversation. They made it look so easy. She was not cut out for this parenting business.

She stabbed a forkful of Cobb salad and checked her phone for new text messages. Nothing. She'd already sent one desperate plea for reinforcements—first to her best friend, Laramie, and then to her brother Drew. Laramie had declined because she had a new puppy to train, but Drew said he'd be by soon.

The door to Angie's Diner swung open, ushering in a blast of cold air along with three guys wearing heavy winter jackets. They paused and stomped the snow off their boots on the mat in the entryway. The first was older and she didn't recognize him, but the second looked familiar—he'd stopped by the store at least once, although she didn't recall his name. The door swung shut behind the third man, and her breath caught as she recognized Gage. He glanced her way and their eyes met, sending a jolt of electricity ricocheting through her.

Connor chose that exact moment to swivel in his high chair and survey the new arrivals, too.

Uh-oh. Skye braced for his reaction once he saw Gage. Just as she feared, Connor pointed and squealed so loud most of the folks in the restaurant turned to see what all the fuss was about.

An embarrassing heat flushed Skye's skin as Gage spoke briefly to his friends before making his way toward her.

"Hey." He stopped beside their table and smiled, making her pulse stutter while Connor took his screeching to a whole new level. "What's up, buddy?"

Connor offered him a soggy fry.

Gage laughed and politely declined. "No, thanks. You can keep it."

The weight of every curious stare in the restaurant made Skye want to crawl under the table. This scene unfolding would give the whole town something to talk about.

Gage shifted his gaze back to her. "Your mom doing all right?"

"Yeah, she's meeting with her book club in the back room." Skye angled her head toward the far end of the restaurant. "I had the crazy idea that I could fly solo with this one tonight."

"Aw, I'm sure he's a great wingman." Gage shoved his hands in his pockets. "I better catch up with the guys. See you next week?"

"Oh, I meant to ask you—would you like to come over on Sunday afternoon? We're having a small party for Connor at four. It's his birthday."

Surprise flickered in Gage's eyes. "Yeah. Of course."

"Perfect." She smiled, relieved he hadn't objected. "See you then."

"Catch you later, dude." Gage waved and walked away.

Connor's gaze tracked him, and then his expression crumpled and he burst into tears.

Not again. Panic welled as Skye tried to counteract his meltdown. She reached for a packet of crackers from the container in the center of the table and ripped it open.

"Here. Want to try a cracker?"

He batted it from her hand while his face deepened to a shade of dark pink. Wow, he was angry.

She tried offering him his sippy cup of apple juice mixed with water, but he pushed that away, too. Her appetite had waned, so she slid her plate aside and reached over to unbuckle Connor's straps. Maybe if she held him, he'd calm down. If that didn't help, she'd have to interrupt Mom's meeting and get them both in the car somehow.

"Need a hand?"

Skye glanced up as Drew slid into the chair opposite hers.

"I've never been so happy to see you in my life." She lifted Connor from his chair and handed him to her brother. "Here."

"Connor, my man. What's the problem?" Drew gently suspended Connor in the air and made a silly face.

Startled, Connor paused his tirade and reached for the bill of Drew's navy-blue-and-orange Broncos cap.

"Are you a Broncos fan?" Drew pulled Connor close and let him grab the edge of the hat. "You'll fit right in around here."

Skye slumped in her chair and took a long sip of her

iced tea. How could one little person's temper tantrum ruffle her feathers so easily?

Maybe this has nothing to do with Connor.

She crunched on a piece of ice and dismissed the idea as quickly as it pinged through her mind. Her frazzled state had nothing to do with seeing Gage.

"Who was that you were speaking to before I got here?" Drew asked, his gaze roaming the restaurant behind her.

"Gage Westbrook. He's the guy I told you about—Connor's dad's friend."

"That's right. I ran his background check. Squeaky-clean. Does he still want to spend time with Connor?" Drew shifted his attention back to Connor and puffed out his cheeks while crossing his eyes, which made the little boy giggle and squeeze Drew's face between his hands.

"He already has."

"Really." Drew pulled back from Connor's grasp and studied her. "How's that going?"

She shrugged. "He had dinner with us, and he played with Connor. I guess it went well."

"Seriously?"

She sighed. "Yes. Seriously. Why?"

"No reason."

His line of questioning made her uneasy. What had he heard? "You seem surprised. What are you not telling me?"

"Nothing."

"Drew. If there's something I need to know, please—"

"Skye, relax. I'm just making conversation." Drew braced Connor against his shoulder and patted his back awkwardly. "What else is he doing, besides hanging out with you?"

"We're not *hanging out*." Skye glared at him. "I'm at the store when he's with Mom and Connor."

"Right." Drew waggled his eyebrows. "Would you hang out if he asked?"

"Don't make me sorry I invited you here." She balled up her paper napkin and flung it at him.

He easily deflected it. "Ha. You begged me."

She sighed and braced her chin on her hand. "You're right. Connor was wearing me out. Next time I'll ask Mom to find a friend to bring her to book club."

"Speaking of Mom, how do you think she's doing?"

"With her knee? As well as can be expected. I think she'll be able to live independently by the time I go back to Denver."

Drew frowned. "Possibly."

"What's wrong? You look worried."

"Even though it's only February, I'm wondering what your long-term plan is with this little guy, that's all."

She leaned across the table and lowered her voice. "I can't stay here forever. That was never the plan. I'm going back to my job right after Easter."

"That's less than two months from now. What will happen to Connor?"

"Maybe I'll take him with me and enroll him in a day care close to my apartment."

Drew's brow furrowed. "Are you sure? That's a huge commitment."

Her stomach twisted in an anxious knot. "I'm not sure, but we don't have a lot of other options. What if McKenna doesn't come back?"

His cheeseburger sat like a rock in his stomach. Nothing against Angie's Diner—the appetizers, burger and fries he'd ordered all tasted great. The reason for his discomfort had everything to do with the man sitting across from Skye on the other side of the restaurant, with Connor snuggled happily in his lap, while she leaned across the table, clearly engaged in meaningful conversation. The whole scenario aggravated him. And he hated to admit it.

"So how do you know Skye?"

Dane's pointed question rammed into Gage's careful introspection. He reached for his soda to keep his gaze from wandering her way again. "I'm a friend of the family's."

"Is that right?" Dane's lips twitched. "Small world."

"How so?"

Dane shrugged and helped himself to one of Gage's fries. "'Cause you haven't quit staring at her since we sat down, it must be—"

"I'm not staring."

"What would you call it, then?"

Gage's scalp prickled. "The baby was making a scene. I felt bad for her."

"Why don't you offer to help her out?" Dane glanced over his shoulder, then back at Gage, and feigned a sad expression. "Oh. Too bad. Somebody beat you to it."

Gage bit back a terse reply. Dane didn't mean any harm. This was tame compared to some of the razzing he'd endured from his navy buddies. He still wasn't going to tell Dane why he cared about Connor. Or Skye.

"Judging by the way you're not staring, I'm guessing you're single?" Dane asked.

Gage nodded and reached for his soda. "You?"

"Yep."

Shocker. Gage drained the last of his soda and set the plastic cup down.

"What made you leave the navy?"

He scrubbed his fingers along his jaw while he caught a glimpse of Skye's new friend kissing the top of Connor's head. Gage's chest tightened. Who *was* that guy? Dragging his gaze back to meet Dane's, he forced himself to sound casual. "I didn't feel the need to reenlist, and this seemed like the right time to try something new."

"Huh. Did you like it?" Dane rattled the ice in his own cup, then flagged the waitress down for a refill.

"Most of the time." He had enjoyed his years in the service. Even the mundane routines when they were in port, struggling through another physical fitness test or filling out paperwork—he'd thrived on the order and clear expectations. But when he'd made a selfish decision that ultimately cost his best friend his life, he'd suddenly loathed his role.

No need to go there tonight. That wasn't exactly something he wanted to reveal, especially if he wanted a permanent job with Alta Vista.

Max sat to Gage's left, swapping stories with a few other guys who'd joined them. They didn't seem to be in a hurry to finish their meals and go home. He stifled a sigh and tried to focus on what Max was talking about. He didn't want to leave before Skye anyway, or he'd have to walk past her table to get to the door. Part of him wanted to see how long her mystery man stuck around.

Dane must've given up on interrogating him, because he shifted his attention to the guy next to him, and before long they were engaged in a lengthy debate about the Rockies baseball team and their prospects for spring training. Normally Gage could hold his own in a conversation about professional sports, but tonight he was way too distracted.

And mad at himself for his acute awareness of Skye's presence. What happened to just being acquaintances with a common goal? In less than an hour he'd already caved on his resolve not to care. The guy holding Connor smiled and even though her back was to him, Gage imagined Skye revealing that beautiful smile of hers. He grabbed his cup and crunched on another mouthful of ice.

Dane shot him an amused look, but Gage ignored him and deliberately shifted in his seat toward Max. If he didn't pay attention to what was happening at Skye's table, maybe he'd have some hope of reining in his irrational thoughts.

A few minutes later, a group of ladies emerged from the back room, laughing as they moved at a slow pace to keep up with one woman using a walker. Mrs. Tomlinson. The parking lot outside was slick. Should she be using a walker to get to the car?

Oh brother. *Stop caring, remember?* He palmed the back of his neck. Full of opinions about what was best for Skye's family, when he really had no business getting involved. They were taking great care of Connor, and minus a few tantrums, he seemed to be thriving.

Why couldn't he leave well enough alone?

Mrs. Tomlinson made her way to Skye's table. Based on her wide smile and the way her hand touched the shoulder of Skye's mystery man, she was thrilled to see him. So they knew each other well. Interesting. Gage couldn't help but watch as Skye stood, lifted Connor into her arms and fumbled with putting his knit hat and jacket on. Mrs. Tomlinson moved toward the door of the diner, while Skye trailed behind, struggling to hold on to a wiggly Connor while shouldering the diaper bag, too.

The man walked behind her, then hurried to open the door for Mrs. Tomlinson. When he pressed his hand to Skye's back and gently guided her outside, Gage's stomach clenched in an ugly knot.

While it wasn't any of his business who Skye dated, Gage wasn't going to let just any guy get close to Connor without asking questions. If Gage was going to keep his promise to Ryan, didn't he owe it to his best friend to inquire about who was allowed into Connor's world?

Chapter Five

"You have polished those blinds to perfection. What gives?" Laramie Chambers, Skye's best friend, sat on Mom's living room floor wrapping Connor's birthday gifts.

"Nothing." Skye swabbed her microfiber cloth across the next row of cream-colored faux wood blinds. "Don't most people clean house before guests come over?"

"This is a birthday party for a one-year-old. You've known all the guests for most of your life. I don't think they'll notice—or care—if there's a little bit of dust."

"I'll notice."

The subtle crinkling of wrapping paper followed by the crisp slice of the scissors answered back. Laramie was too kind to say what she was thinking. She'd been her closest friend since seventh grade and was quite skilled at recognizing Skye's coping strategies.

Laramie was right—they'd intentionally planned a small, low-key gathering so as not to overwhelm Connor. There was still one guest in particular she was concerned about—one she hardly knew at all. That was what was driving her compulsion to clean, because that was what she did when she was worked up—created order out of chaos. It soothed her. So what if most women their age didn't spend their Saturday nights dusting their mother's blinds? Most twentysomething single women she knew didn't have a widowed mother reading quietly in bed down the hall, or someone else's baby asleep in a crib in the next room.

Satisfied the blinds were cleansed of all dust particles, she moved on to purging the wooden coffee table of extra magazines and junk mail. Her thoughts wandered to all the Saturday nights she'd spent out to dinner with friends at one of the trendy restaurants downtown or enjoying a musical at the theater. Lazy weekends doing whatever she wanted and taking her time to prepare for the coming workweek. Since Connor had upended every area of her life, she'd surprisingly spent very little time thinking about the vibrant social life she'd left behind. Her conversation with Drew at the diner last night had her second-guessing her future, though. Could she return to Denver with Connor in tow? What would happen when she severed the bond already forming between Gage and Connor?

"Want to tell me what's really bothering you?"

No. Yes. Skye heaved a sigh and sank onto the couch, a stack of magazines in her hands. "I wish I hadn't told Gage about Connor's party."

Laramie glanced up from the gift she'd just wrapped, her long platinum hair woven in a fishbone-style braid dangling over her shoulder. Her pencil-thin brows tented over her wide-set green eyes. "Told him or invited him? There's a difference, you know."

"Invited. Sort of." She tipped her head back and stared at the ceiling. "It just slipped out before I could think about what I was saying."

"That's rather out of character for you, isn't it?" Laramie's voice carried a teasing lilt.

"I know," Skye groaned. "What am I going to do?"

"About…"

"Gage. Here." Skye pushed to her feet, abandoning the magazines on the couch cushions. "More than I want him to be."

There. She'd said it. Somehow honesty had done little to ease the familiar anxiety snaring her in its grasp. She crossed to the fireplace and collected the plastic Little People Connor had abandoned on the brick hearth before bath time, then swept them into the woven basket doubling as toy storage.

"I'm confused," Laramie said. "You don't want him here at all, or just not at Connor's party?"

"Letting him watch Connor, even for a few hours a day, was a difficult decision. It was so unexpected, the way he showed up, claiming this connection to Connor. Then when we saw him at the diner, Connor was giving me a fit, and I—I thought he might be happier if Gage was here for the party tomorrow."

Oh brother. It sounded even more ridiculous when she said it out loud.

"So what are you worried about? Sounds like a thoughtful gesture to me." Laramie slapped a green bow on the gift wrapped in green-and-yellow paper with a tractor pattern. "Do you think it's going to be awkward or something?"

"I'm just—" Skye gnawed on her thumbnail. "What if Connor gets too attached to him?"

Understanding flashed across Laramie's features, as though the proverbial lightbulb had illuminated in her mind. "Connor? Or you?"

Skye shot her a pointed look. "This isn't about me."

"Are you sure about that?"

"Positive."

Mostly.

Sure, he was handsome and if she wasn't careful, those hazel eyes might be her undoing, but she could handle herself. She frequently crossed paths with attractive men when she called on physicians at their offices to pitch a new pharmaceutical product. Keeping Gage at arm's length wasn't an issue.

It was Connor she was worried about. Everything about his life was one big holding pattern. Including Gage. What happened when he started working full-time? Or if McKenna came back and undid all the stability she and Mom had worked hard to establish for Connor? In her effort to help, was she only causing more harm long-term by allowing another person into Connor's world who might not stick around?

"Connor is very young, and he's been through a lot but he's also resilient." Laramie drew her knees to her chest and wrapped her arms around them. "I've worked with a few kids at school who endured childhood trauma and are delightful, well-adjusted teenagers."

Skye valued Laramie's opinion. After growing up in Merritt's Crossing, then coming back after college to teach language arts at the high school and coach volleyball, Laramie had more insight into the resiliency of kids than she did. Still, worry niggled at Skye like a foe she couldn't conquer.

"I—I want some reassurance that this isn't going to wreck him." She stacked the wrapped gifts on the hearth.

"Have you prayed about it?"

No. She swallowed back a snarky response and avoided Laramie's gaze.

"Skye—"

"I know." She held up both palms in self-defense. "You don't need to go there. I've heard it all before."

"Maybe you need to hear it again," Laramie said gently. "Listen, I know you've had a rough time lately. Between a difficult breakup and all your family has endured, I don't blame you for being anxious about the future. Or having trust issues."

Skye's limbs itched with the need to move, and her gaze darted around the room for something else to clean. To straighten. While she welcomed her bestie's advice on almost anything, the trajectory of her insight into Skye's now-dormant relationship with the Lord was most certainly not welcome.

Laramie didn't understand.

"I know what you're thinking," Laramie said, "and you're partially right—I don't fully understand what it's like to have dated a controlling man."

"You're right, that's exactly what I was thinking." Skye spotted a neglected animal cracker under the recliner in the corner and knelt to retrieve it. Short of leaving the room, she couldn't ignore the rest of what Laramie had to say, though. She sank back on her heels and forced herself to look at her friend.

"I know God loves me, Lare. He is all that He claims to be in His word." Her voice wobbled. "But sometimes I just can't figure out what He is doing. My dad was not a perfect man, but why was he killed in a terrible accident? And Connor—he's just a baby. Why does he have to grow up without a father? And why did my uncle—"

"Wait." This time Laramie held up her hand to interrupt, her eyes coated in a fresh sheen of moisture. "We are not alone in our struggles. God is with us for every horrible second."

Emotion tightened Skye's throat. Slowly, she shook her head. "I don't believe that's true."

"God is big enough to handle your doubts and your questions," Laramie said. "Don't be afraid to bring them to Him."

She turned away, intent on finishing her clean sweep of the cozy living room, while she willed fresh tears not to fall. God did still love her, but He seemed to have forgotten her and her family. Just like her dad's short-comings had caused an ongoing dispute. That was why it was up to her to make sure Connor's needs were met. He didn't have a father, either, and she'd do everything in her power to protect him.

After church and an epic shopping trip to the big-box store on the interstate, Gage returned to his apart-ment with groceries and three bags full of gifts for Connor. Once the groceries were put away, he moved to the living room and spread his haul across the glass-topped industrial metal coffee table. A stuffed elephant, four books, a container of small rubber ducks for the tub and one large red plastic barn.

Yeah, he might've gone a little overboard. Skye would not be happy with him if he showed up with his arms full of gifts.

He winced at the mental image of her flashing him a disapproving look. Not that he wanted her to be dis-pleased, but standing in the toy aisle, all he could think about was how much he wished Ryan was there to cele-brate Connor's first birthday, so he'd loaded everything into the shopping cart.

Rubbing his hand across his jaw, he tried to narrow his selection to one gift. It wasn't easy, but he eventu-ally picked the red plastic barn. When he'd visited for dinner, he'd noticed a small container with a half-dozen rubber farm animals. Maybe as Connor became more mobile, he'd progress to playing with the animals and the barn together.

Gage tucked the rest of the gifts back into the bags along with the receipt and stowed them in his coat closet. He'd return them on his next trip. At the store, he'd also spent a ridiculous amount of time in the wrapping paper section, temporarily paralyzed by the options. Honestly, the whole process of wrapping a gift felt daunting. He didn't have much experience. Once or twice as a child, he'd done enough chores for a neighbor to scrounge together a few bucks to buy his mom a gift. Even then, he'd had to make do with a brown paper grocery bag, markers and tape he'd "borrowed" from school to wrap it.

The hazy memory provoked an unexpected ache of loneliness. His mom had done the best she could—he knew that now. But her addiction often overpowered her, and people let her get by with flimsy excuses and empty promises. The ache in his chest deepened at the painful memories of all the birthdays that passed uncelebrated. No cake, no ice cream and definitely no gifts adorned with festive wrapping paper.

On one particular birthday, he'd rushed from his bed in their double-wide trailer, his bare feet skimming across the grungy shag carpeting, hoping with everything in his nine-year-old self that she'd remembered. That this birthday would be different.

Mom had stood at the counter in their tiny kitchen, wearing her faded bathrobe and smoking a cigarette. Only a bright yellow Mylar balloon with a smiley face waited for him.

Hey, baby. Happy birthday.

If he closed his eyes, he could still hear her raspy voice. Still feel the remnant of the hurt and disappointment. Man, he'd wanted to pop that stupid balloon.

He'd spent the next three birthdays in different foster care homes, and by the time he and Mom were reunited, he'd known to keep his expectations low. Dad was out of the picture, and he had learned the hard way that he couldn't count on her, either.

Gage stood and crossed to the closet again, retrieved the new stuffed elephant and carried it back to the living room. As long as he was around, Connor would never experience a birthday like that. What was wrong with a little excessive giving? The poor kid didn't have a mom or a dad. Surely Skye would understand if he brought something on behalf of Ryan.

Skye.

He couldn't ignore all the ways she'd crept into his thoughts since he'd seen her and Connor with that guy at the diner. He'd probably be at the birthday party today, too. Gage gritted his teeth and reached for the gift bags and tissue paper he'd bought instead of wrapping paper. Even though he didn't have a right to care about who she spent time with, it bothered him that they'd looked so comfortable together. It bothered him even more that she'd managed to get under his skin and make him jealous.

He groaned and ripped the plastic off the tissue paper. *Get a grip, dude*. Skye was not interested in hearing his opinions about what was best for Connor.

While he'd given himself that same pep talk multiple times, the message didn't seem to be sinking in. Or else he was too stubborn to admit he'd have to accept that other people—other men—would be involved in Connor's life, as well.

But he didn't have to like it.

The first sheet of fragile paper tore in his big hands, and he crumpled it in disgust and tossed it on the cream-colored carpet. Wasn't there a YouTube video for this? He picked up his phone and scrolled until he found help in the form of a video tutorial. Somehow the woman made it look effortless.

Finally, he'd wrestled the tissue paper and gifts into both bags, and it was time to leave.

Outside, wisps of feathery clouds were brushed against a pale blue sky and sunlight reflected off the white snowbanks. He set both gift bags gently on the passenger seat and started his truck. Again, his gaze landed on Ryan, staring back at him from the photograph. Grief tinged with remorse crept in, and Gage hunched forward, pressing his forehead against the steering wheel.

This was really happening—Connor's first birthday. Without Ryan or McKenna.

If you hadn't been so careless, maybe things would be different.

The harsh words knifed at him. Even though he'd conjured them on his own, they stung as if spoken aloud. It was true. His actions had deprived a sweet baby of ever knowing his father. There weren't enough birthday presents in the world to make up for that. The weight of the guilt almost made him want to go back inside and skip the whole thing. His throat constricted, and he swallowed hard, determined to gain control of his emotions.

He couldn't stay home. Not just because he had gifts to bring. Ryan would want him to be at Connor's party.

Gage straightened, whispered a prayer for strength and made the short drive to the Tomlinsons' neighborhood. As he approached their house, he counted five vehicles parked on the street, although none looked familiar. Easing his truck to the curb, he turned off the engine and stared at the front door. Man, he wasn't great at parties. The small talk, standing around and balancing a plate of food, trying to pretend he was having a good time—anxiety rippled through him.

C'mon. Don't be a wimp. You've got this.

He grabbed the gifts, climbed out of his truck and strode toward the front porch. Honoring his promise to Ryan meant participating in Connor's major life events, even if that made him uncomfortable. He wiped his clammy palm on his jeans and then knocked softly, in case Connor was still napping. When the door swung open, he expected Skye, but a vaguely familiar guy greeted him on the other side.

"Hey, come on in. You must be Gage." He grinned and stepped back. "Skye's told me a lot about you. I'm Drew, by the way."

The guy from the diner. Great. Jealousy slithered in and took up residence. He forced a cool smile and shook Drew's hand, trying to mentally smother the ugly emotions. He hated the thought of competing for Connor's attention, and even worse, he hated acknowledging that he was jealous of another guy being involved in Connor's life. It was going to be a long party.

Skye dunked the glass mixing bowl in the hot soapy water and reached for the sponge.

She needed a minute. A minute to scrub something until it sparkled. A minute away from Gage and his big shoulders and hazel eyes and smooth voice that kept reeling her toward him like an invisible thread.

Gage had arrived at Connor's party less than fifteen

minutes ago, and already she was hiding in the kitchen, stalling while Drew chatted him up.

Honestly, what was she—twelve? Her skin flushed at the thought of her family and friends watching her try to ignore him for the rest of the evening.

Through the kitchen window, headlights illuminated the gathering darkness as a car approached and then slowed at the end of the driveway. Skye sucked in a breath and the bowl slid from her hands, landing in the dishwater with a clunk.

McKenna?

All day, Skye kept a close watch on her phone, flinching with every chime and notification. Wouldn't McKenna at least acknowledge her son's first birthday? No calls, texts or instant messages had arrived yet. Skye had scrolled through McKenna's social media accounts, too, but her cousin hadn't posted anything.

The car sped up and disappeared around the corner.

Deflated, Skye released a breath and leaned against the counter. A hollow ache filled her chest. She hadn't realized until this moment how much hope she'd invested in McKenna coming back in time for Connor's birthday.

"Everything okay?" Gage's deep voice enveloped her.

"Trying to clean up a little before we serve dinner." She tried for a smile, but it wobbled and did not go unnoticed.

A ridge formed in his normally flawless brow. "Anything I can do to help?"

In his gray sweater with the sleeves pushed up to reveal chiseled forearms, and his athletic frame filling the space between the counter's edge and the wall, her pulse ratcheted up a notch.

Quick! Assign him a task.

But her mouth was dry, and her eyes wandered from his gold-flecked gaze to the hint of a five o'clock shadow hugging his jawline—

"Skye?" His eyes searched her face. Without warning, he reached up and gently grazed her cheek with the pad of his thumb. For a hot second, she longed to lean into his touch. The warmth of his gaze pulled her in, making her forget how much it had cost her the last time she'd let down her guard.

Warning bells chimed in her head and she quickly stepped back.

"Sorry." He shoved his hands in the back pockets of his jeans. "You had soap on your face."

"I—I need to make sure my brother brought his camera." It was a lame excuse, and only half-true, but she had to put some space between the two of them. She let her gaze dart around the kitchen, avoiding eye contact.

"Your brother?"

"The guy who answered the door. Didn't he introduce himself?" She lifted a platter of deviled eggs from the counter and willed Gage to move out of her way.

"Yeah, I just…didn't make the connection." His smile was tight as he reached for the platter. "Can I carry that for you?"

"Put it on the table, next to the coleslaw." Instantly, she regretted the bossiness in her tone. "Please." She tacked on the word as an afterthought, flung halfheartedly toward his retreating back. Even in dark-washed jeans and a sweater, Gage's impressive stature—no doubt honed from his years in the navy—was hard to ignore. Since he couldn't see her, and she was blocked from her family's line of sight as well, Skye allowed herself to admire him—just for a second.

Until he pivoted and caught her staring.

Busted. He arched one eyebrow and then set the deviled eggs on the table.

She slipped around the corner and into the living room, where Uncle Milt and Aunt Linda had just arrived. She'd never been so happy to see her mother's sister and her husband.

"Thank you so much for coming," Skye said as Aunt Linda carried a large casserole pan toward the dining room table. "I've been thinking about your barbecued pulled pork all day."

"We wouldn't miss it, sweetie." Aunt Linda lowered the pan to the table, then glanced around the room. "Now, where is that adorable baby?"

Right on cue, Connor giggled, drawing the attention of everyone in the room. In his blue jeans and red T-shirt, he sat in the middle of the floor, babbling happily to Skye's younger brother, Jack. Much to her surprise, he'd decided to come to the party after all. Mom had been convinced he'd find a reason not to. In his crisp, white button-down with the pearl snaps, Wrangler jeans and cowboy boots, he looked...good. As if he'd tried to impress someone. But who?

Skye glanced to the sofa where Laramie sat between her parents, her gaze riveted on Jack, as well. Huh. Interesting. They'd definitely have a few things to discuss later.

Connor held out a red bow he'd managed to rip from one of his gifts prematurely, and Jack took it, then set it gently on Connor's head. When it slid off, more belly laughs ensued.

"Oh my." Aunt Linda smiled and propped her hands on her ample hips. "Isn't he the cutest thing? You must be having the time of your life taking care of him."

Skye opened her mouth to respond but swallowed back the harsh words before they spilled out.

No. She wasn't having a good time. Connor had a lot of needs and she struggled to meet them. This wasn't what she'd signed up for when she'd agreed to come home and help. This boy belonged with a mother and father who loved him and knew what to do when he seemed to cry for no reason at all. But Connor had already lost his father, and his mother... Could her cousin ever be a dependable caregiver?

Skye pushed the nagging doubts away. She had a house full of people to tend to.

The pleasant hum of conversation filtered through the cozy space, and the aroma of Aunt Linda's barbecued pork made her stomach growl.

Connor's exuberant chatter drew her attention, and she glanced at him, still sitting on the floor surrounded by presents. He lifted both arms toward Gage. Skye's breath hitched. Now, that was one gesture she did understand— he wanted Gage.

"What's up, buddy? Need some help?" Gage's arm brushed against hers as he moved past her and joined Connor and Jack on the floor. While she'd stood there, overanalyzing her struggles with Connor, somehow Gage had moved closer without her noticing. Her traitorous abdomen dispensed another batch of butterflies as she watched Gage and Connor interact.

"Hey, everyone, we're going to let Connor open his presents before we eat," Skye said, quickly granting permission. She could only imagine his disappointment if they asked him to wait any longer.

Connor crawled into Gage's lap, and then Gage handed him a present and helped him rip off the paper. Everyone expressed their approval while Gage encouraged Connor to open the next gift. Skye's heart expanded in her chest. They were really cute together. She grabbed her phone and sank to the floor nearby, eager to capture the moment with a photo. Maybe she'd get to share the image with McKenna someday.

When the presents were opened, Gage glanced at Skye for direction. "What next?"

"Let me ask my uncle Milt to say the blessing." She pushed to her feet and tugged on her uncle's chambray sleeve. "Uncle Milt, will you please pray so we can eat?"

"Of course." Uncle Milt's weathered skin wrinkled as he grinned, and his pale blue eyes flitted toward Gage. "First, how about you introduce us to your beau?"

All eyes swung in her direction and an expectant silence blanketed the room.

"Right. I mean, no, he's—he's not—" Flustered, she glanced at Gage. He wore a smile that rivaled Uncle Milt's. Clearly, he was enjoying watching her squirm.

Cheeks flaming, she forced a smile and addressed the rest of the group. "Thank you for coming to Connor's party, everyone. This is our new friend, Gage Westbrook. He moved here to finish his certification to become a wind energy technician. We just met recently because he happens to be a good friend of Connor's father. Now Uncle Milt is going to pray, and then we can eat."

There. A brief introduction that clarified his status as definitively in the friend zone. Where he belonged.

Gage's afternoon with Connor wasn't going as well as he'd hoped.

Connor sat beside him on the living room floor, his lower lip protruding while he rubbed both chubby fists against his eyes. He hadn't napped nearly as long as

Skye's detailed notes said he should. Mrs. Tomlinson had warned him before she'd retreated to her room for her own nap that Connor might be a little grumpy.

"Do you want to play with your new toys?" Gage slid the red plastic barn across the carpet toward Connor.

He pushed it away and started to fuss.

Oh boy. Gage gritted his teeth and looked around for the collection of colorful rubber animals he'd noticed the first night he'd stopped by. He found them in a basket nearby and dumped them on the carpet.

"Do you like cows?" Gage gently walked the black-and-white cow up Connor's leg. "Moo."

Connor amped up the tears, his face darkening from pink to red as he scooted out of Gage's reach.

"Okay, that's a negative on the farm animals." Gage quickly put them away. Man, this was a big change from the birthday party, when Connor acted like Gage could do no wrong. Anxiety hummed in his veins and he looked around for an option that might soothe the baby.

Thankfully Mrs. Tomlinson had changed Connor's diaper when he woke up, so scratch that from the list of reasons Connor kept crying. He reached for an orange dump truck with a gray plastic rock in the back.

"Check this out, Connor." Gage drove it across the carpet and tried to make an authentic engine noise.

Connor just wailed louder.

"You're right, that sound I made was pretty lame." Gage angled the truck toward the fireplace and set it on the hearth. He palmed the back of his neck. Why was he so bad at this?

Turning, he reached for Connor and scooped him awkwardly into his arms. "Come here, little dude. What's the matter?"

Tears clung to Connor's eyelashes and moisture

dampened his cheeks. Gage's heart fisted as Connor drew a ragged breath, then continued to cry. There had to be something that would help calm him. Gage stood slowly and walked toward the sliding glass door beside the dining room table.

"Let's look out the window." Maybe a peek outside might distract him? Gage shifted Connor in his arms so he could see the backyard. Remnants of snow from the last storm still lingered on the ground, and the cloudy gray sky hinted there was more winter weather to come. A few birds and squirrels scampered about.

"Look at the squirrels, Connor." Gage pressed his finger to the glass. "Do you see them?"

Connor stopped crying and his big blue eyes widened as he made a few sounds Gage couldn't interpret.

"What else do you see?" Gage gently patted Connor's back, wishing he could take him outside. The green one-piece outfit Connor wore had long sleeves, but he only had socks on and Gage had no idea where his jacket and shoes might be. If Mrs. Tomlinson had managed to sleep through all the crying, he didn't want to disturb her to ask.

There was so much comfort in fresh air, though. Or maybe just the change in perspective helped. Memories of his own childhood flooded back, reminding him of the times he'd slipped outside in a desperate attempt to escape the anxiety and fear of his parents' neglect and, later, his latest temporary foster care placement.

Connor babbled another string of unintelligible sounds, pulling Gage back to the present.

"I know. There's a lot to look at, isn't there?" He didn't really know how to talk to a one-year-old, and he felt a little silly at the moment. If his comments kept the crying to a minimum, though, he'd keep chatting.

Connor pointed toward the yard, then glanced at Gage and smiled. The tension in Gage's shoulders loosened. His frustration over the crying was no match for that innocent blue-eyed stare and toothy grin. Or the sweet scent that accompanied Connor. Gage smiled back, and Connor responded by resting his head against Gage's shoulder and heaving a deep sigh.

Gage's breath hitched. He wasn't quite prepared for the sudden display of affection. Thoughts of Ryan invaded, and he willed the tightness in his throat to go away. He couldn't bring his friend back, but he'd do everything in his power to build a relationship with Ryan's son.

Gage shifted and glanced at the clock on the wall. Three fifteen. Skye's instructions mentioned an afternoon snack of dry cereal and a sippy cup of apple juice. He didn't relish the thought of ruining the peaceful moment, but he knew better than to ignore her expectations. Especially on his first day with Connor.

"Are you ready for a snack?" Gage asked as he turned toward the high chair nearby.

Connor raised his head and looked around. No crying yet. That was good, right? Gage gently lowered him into the chair, buckled the straps and then adjusted the tray, just like he'd watched Skye do at dinner last week. There. Nothing to it.

Feeling more confident, he hurried to get the plastic container with the dry cereal and the cup of juice while Connor entertained himself by clapping his hands, then squealing with delight.

A few minutes later, Connor happily munched on his Cheerios, while Gage sat at the table and stifled a yawn. Sleep had eluded him last night, and he'd tossed and turned, snapshots of his evening spent at Connor's party still playing on an endless loop in his mind. Two days had passed. He should have powered through these convoluted emotions by now. Skye, her close-knit family, the bittersweet experience of celebrating Connor's birthday while pretending not to notice he didn't have any parents had churned him up inside. Made him do things he normally wouldn't—like touching her cheek when he'd found her alone in the kitchen.

Probably shouldn't have done that.

Someone or something must've hurt her deeply, because she'd skittered away as quickly as possible. He didn't imagine the chemistry arcing between them, though, and he couldn't ignore his own sense of relief once he figured out the guy from the diner was her brother.

He'd tried to speak with Skye privately—to let her know he hadn't meant to overstep her boundaries—but celebrating Connor took center stage for the rest of the evening. Although he'd stuck around to help clean up, her boisterous family and friends made meaningful conversation difficult. He shook his head, still smiling at the mischievous gleam in her uncle's eyes, and the ways her brothers provoked her for their own amusement. The party made him both envious and terrified at the same time. Skye and her family finished each other's sentences and dished out plenty of good-natured ribbing, yet their long history together and commitment to one another gave him the urge to run. It was too much. Too much intensity. Too much loyalty. Even if they weren't all related, the guests at the party lived in a densely woven web of connection and shared experience.

His status as an outsider was painfully obvious. Yet his desperate longing to keep his promise to Ryan and now to Connor, and his changing feelings for Skye, had kept him at the party. And motivated him to give his very best effort while caring for the little boy. If he was honest, he longed to be included, to build those rock-solid relationships, but his years in foster care made it difficult to trust people. Would he ever be able to have a family of his own and not live in fear of abandonment?

Chapter Six

Early Wednesday morning, Gage poured the contents of his smoothie from the blender into a tall plastic cup, then jabbed a straw into the thick mixture and took a sip. Meh. Not his best work. Wasting food was practically a criminal offense in his opinion, so he'd drink it anyway.

The laminate floor was cold against his bare feet as he crossed to his kitchen table and sat down in front of his laptop. It wasn't even 6 a.m., and he'd already subjected himself to a punishing workout in his apartment complex's fitness center, showered and made breakfast—all in a desperate attempt to avoid the email sitting unread in his inbox.

Somewhere around four this morning, he'd woken up, plagued with doubt about whether or not he was doing the right thing—dropping into Connor's life like this. Yesterday afternoon got off to a rocky start, but then Connor snuggled up close, and the surge of affection blindsided Gage.

Maybe this was just the same old fear taunting him. It wasn't a surprise when his ex-girlfriend told him he was emotionally unavailable. But that didn't make it any easier to hear.

Or admit that she was right. He didn't want to be alone forever. Yet the unpredictability of these big emotions did scare him because he knew how much it hurt when relationships fell apart. Connor's ability to sneak past his defenses, as well as his unmistakable attraction toward Skye, left him feeling vulnerable. And he didn't like it. Not one bit.

Frustrated, he'd reached for his phone to find a podcast or some music to help him fall back asleep when a message from Ryan's parents unexpectedly greeted him. Although he'd tried to pretend he hadn't seen it, the sickening lurch in his gut had propelled him out of bed and kept him in perpetual motion. Resistance was futile, though. He couldn't avoid it much longer. His heart rate quickened as his finger hovered over the keyboard, poised to open the message.

Dear Gage,

We hope this message finds you well and thriving. Gerald and I are getting by, although time has not healed all wounds, as they say. We still can't believe he is gone. I'm writing to you in hopes that you can help us sort out a troubling development. It has come to our attention that Ryan has a son. This wasn't something he'd disclosed to us. As you can imagine, we are both shocked and saddened to learn of our only grandchild in this manner. When you have a few minutes, would you please give us a call? You are one of our limited sources of information, and we'd desperately like to know more about this baby and where he might be.

Sincerely,

Gerald and Irene Simmons

Blood pounded in his ears as Gage pushed to his feet, eager to get away from his laptop. They didn't know? How was that possible? He strode to the window in the living room and stared out into the early-morning sky streaked in rich shades of orange, proclaiming the sun's imminent arrival.

Ryan had talked about his parents often, and his all-American experience in the affluent Chicago suburbs was the exact opposite of Gage's erratic childhood in Texas. Although Gage had only seen Gerald and Irene twice, once when they visited briefly in San Diego and again at Ryan's funeral, their love and devotion to their only child was obvious. While Ryan had described them as quite conservative, Gage assumed Ryan had eventually disclosed his relationship with McKenna and even told them about Connor.

She didn't come to the funeral. He mentally connected the dots. That might explain one reason why they weren't aware. While Ryan might not have told his parents about McKenna or her pregnancy, they had the right to know more about their only grandchild.

Gage scrubbed his palm across his face. Worse than the knowledge that Gerald and Irene were just now finding out about Connor was the realization that he'd have to tell Skye. What if she was happy about locating more of Connor's relatives? Would she advocate for Connor to go and live with his grandparents?

Stop.

He drew a deep breath and forced himself not to overreact. Gerald and Irene only wanted more information, and he needed to do the right thing and answer promptly.

Gage turned away from the window and went back to the kitchen table and his laptop. His fingers trembled as he typed his response confirming Connor's existence and where he lived. While Gage wanted what was best for Connor, which was a permanent home with two loving parents, the possibility of the little boy getting caught in the volatile process of finding a forever family lodged an icy ball in Gage's gut. He remembered well the heartache of his own uncertain childhood and didn't want Connor to suffer the same way.

Oh, the crying.

She'd tried everything. Nothing helped Connor feel better. Poor little guy. He seemed miserable. Skye paced the short hallway between the bedrooms and the living room, the distraught baby nestled against her shoulder. Her arms ached from holding him, but when she tried to put him back in his crib, he screamed louder.

They'd walked endless loops around the house, from the kitchen and dining room, then back down the short hallway. Judging by the light glowing from behind the living room drapes, morning wasn't far away. Fatigue made her limbs feel heavy. What she wouldn't give to lie down and sleep. He'd started crying around 2 a.m. and hadn't really stopped.

She pressed her hand to his forehead again. "Oh, you still feel too warm." She'd already given him the last dose of fever-reducing medicine left in the tiny bottle. Why wasn't it helping? And how was she supposed to know if he needed a different medication?

Her chest tightened at the harsh reminder of all she had to learn about caring for someone so small and helpless. If he didn't settle down in the next few minutes, she'd call the pediatrician. Even though the office didn't open until nine, she could still leave a message.

Connor paused and drew a deep breath.

Skye stopped walking and leaned away from him to study his cherubic face. His eyelids drooped slightly and then he jammed his thumb in his mouth. Skye held her breath. Was his fever breaking? He nuzzled his cheek against her shoulder again, and a few seconds later, she felt his body relax.

"Finally," she whispered and resumed her slow path toward the living room. She was tempted to put him down in his crib, but feared he'd only wake up and start crying all over again. It'd be better to keep him in motion until she was certain he'd fallen asleep.

Mom's bedroom door opened, and Skye turned slowly.

Mom hesitated in the doorway, tightened the sash on her light blue robe, then moved toward Skye, pushing the silver walker in front of her.

"I'm sorry," Skye whispered. "I was hoping he wouldn't bother you."

"I was awake anyway." Mom raked one hand through her short salt-and-pepper curls. "What's the matter?"

"He has a fever." Skye's gaze traveled to Mom's knee. "Why aren't you sleeping well? Is your knee bothering you?"

"My knee feels all right. I haven't slept well since your dad died." She offered a weak smile. "Not used to sleeping alone, I guess."

"I'm sorry to hear that." Skye resumed her gentle swaying, while her chest ached at the mention of Dad. He'd been gone a little over a year. After more than thirty years of marriage, it was understandable that Mom hadn't adjusted to his absence. They were all still feeling the pain his loss inflicted.

"Want some coffee?" Mom steered her walker toward the kitchen.

"Please." Skye followed her, gently shifting Connor in her arms. Although her back and arms screamed for relief, the pleasant sound of his even breathing motivated her to keep holding him. She'd do whatever it took to keep him asleep for as long as possible.

"I have that appointment with my surgeon today at nine," Mom said. "Want me to call and reschedule?"

Oh no. Skye winced. She'd forgotten. "No, I—I can take you."

Mom's brown eyes flitted to Connor. "With a sick child?"

"We don't really have a choice. You need to keep that appointment. How about Drew or Jack?"

"Drew is on highway patrol today, and Jack is likely swamped. One of his IT clients had a security breach."

"He can't spare two hours to take you to the doctor?"

Her mother continued scooping coffee into the coffee maker.

Skye clamped her mouth shut. Drew was helpful when he wasn't working as a sheriff's deputy, but other than Connor's birthday party, Jack had only stopped by to visit once since their mom's surgery. He lived less than an hour away, and he conveniently found plenty of reasons to keep busy. Mom said it was his coping strategy. Coming to the house reminded him too much of Dad.

Frustrated, she heaved a sigh, which prompted a pathetic whimper from Connor. Skye stiffened, then rubbed his back gently and made a soft shushing noise like her mother had taught her.

"Gage seems nice." Mom shot her a hopeful glance. "We could ask him."

"Mom." Skye tried to keep the irritation from her

voice. "We aren't going to ask Gage to drive you to the doctor's office."

"Why not?"

"Because he's already helping us this afternoon. Besides, I'm supposed to open the store at ten, so asking him to drive you doesn't solve my child care problem."

"Honey, it's all right if the store doesn't open on time. Or at all. Things happen. Most folks will understand."

Skye bit back a sharp answer. Wasn't Dad honest with her about the store's precarious finances? Why didn't Mom realize they couldn't afford to lose any sales?

"I'm still not asking him to drive you to your appointment. What about Aunt Linda? She said she'd be glad to help you."

"I don't mind calling her, although she lives farther away than Gage. We'll be cutting it close if I have to wait for her to get ready and then come over."

Skye refused to back down. "Why don't you call her right now? I'll stay home with Connor until Gage gets here and then open the store late."

Mom studied her with a pinched expression. "All right." She pushed her walker toward the cordless telephone mounted on the kitchen wall. "I still don't understand why you're being so skeptical about Gage. He was great with Connor yesterday. If you'll let him babysit, why can't he give me a ride to the doctor?"

Skye ignored her and gingerly shifted Connor's weight as she took a mug from the cabinet. While Mom spoke to Aunt Linda, Skye swayed back and forth and waited while the coffee brewed. How could she explain to Mom that she couldn't afford not to be skeptical? She'd been wooed one too many times by a handsome guy with a megawatt smile. A man who'd transformed into an outspoken control freak behind closed doors. This time she'd be smarter. More aware. The walls of her still-fragile heart were fortified against smooth-talking men. She wouldn't make the same mistake again.

"Take it easy. Let me help you." Gage held Mrs. Tomlinson's elbow and carefully helped her from the floor to the sofa.

She grimaced, her face pinched with concentration and perspiration dotting her forehead.

"You've got this." He held his breath until she was safely in a seated position. While she'd probably done her leg-strengthening exercises numerous times, it still made him nervous seeing her try to get up without assistance. Gage feared Skye would clobber him if anything happened to her mother on his watch.

Right on cue, his phone chimed from his back pocket. Most likely another text from Skye. She'd sent three already in the two hours she'd been at the furniture store.

Mrs. Tomlinson gave him the side-eye. "She's checking up on us again, isn't she?"

"Yes, ma'am. I believe so."

"That girl is going to wear herself out." She reached for her water bottle and twisted off the cap.

"What do you mean?" Gage pulled his phone out and sat down on the opposite end of the sofa.

"I don't make a habit of talking about my children behind their backs, and I certainly can't blame her for getting worked up. We've got a lot going on." Mrs. Tomlinson paused and took a long sip. "On the other hand, I'd love to see her simmer down a notch, you know?"

Gage couldn't hide his smile. He hadn't expected her to speak so candidly.

"That look on your face tells me you agree."

"She does seem stressed. I'm sure she's trying to do what's best for the people she loves, though."

He glanced at his screen while Mrs. Tomlinson took another sip of water.

How is Connor doing? Does he still have a fever? Did he take a long nap? Has Mom finished her exercises? Please remind her to ice afterward.

Oh boy. He sighed and set his phone on the coffee table without responding. Maybe she did need to simmer down a notch. Connor was still napping, and Mrs. Tomlinson appeared to be doing everything she was supposed to.

"I'm sorry." Mrs. Tomlinson shot him an apologetic glance. "I shouldn't have said that. You're right, she is trying to do what's best. She's been very good about taking care of her family, especially her cousin."

The hair on Gage's arm stood on end. "How so?"

"My husband was a good man, and he thought he was doing the right thing for the family at the time, but he and his brother, McKenna's father, had a blowout over our furniture store." She pressed her lips together. "My husband was willed the store by their father, and Kenny, my brother-in-law, was much better at working with his hands. He could build a table and chairs that were absolute works of art. Most of the furniture in this house, he built. Anyway, Kenny was so upset and accused us of swindling him out of the family business. He—he took his own life a few years back, and we have always blamed ourselves."

Gage's chest tightened. "I'm sorry for your loss."

"Thank you." She patted his arm. "McKenna was always a spirited child, and her daddy's girl. She got away with a lot, growing up. Mostly silly stuff. We called her mischievous and headstrong. Never imagined it would come to this. The rift in our family and then his death wrecked her."

Her words pricked at lingering wounds. He could relate. The loss of his own parents and then Ryan's accident had done a number on him emotionally. Palming the back of his neck, Gage tried to process this new layer to an already complicated scenario. "If your family was fighting over the store, then why did she leave Connor with you and Skye? As payback?"

Mrs. Tomlinson sighed and tucked a strand of her hair behind her ear. "I don't know why exactly. I suspect she knew motherhood was not her thing, and it isn't really Skye's thing, either, but I think she knew Skye was dependable. She wouldn't turn her away."

"Did you just say motherhood isn't Skye's thing?"

"Skye has zero interest in being a mother." Mrs. Tomlinson studied him. "She has a good heart, but I know she's only here right now because she loves us and can't bear to see us struggling."

Gage could only stare at Mrs. Tomlinson. He had so many questions. The muffled sound of Connor crying broke the silence and he quickly stood.

"Gage—"

"I'd better check on him." Gage skirted the coffee table and strode toward Connor's room, his mind racing. *Skye has zero interest in being a mother.* Why did he find that so hard to believe? And what did it mean for Connor? If she didn't really want him, was she only caring for him out of guilt and obligation? What happened when she'd finally reached her limit?

He quietly pushed open the door of Connor's room

and found the boy had pulled himself to a standing position inside his crib. Tears tracked down his red cheeks, and he stretched out both arms over the crib rail while repeating a string of consonants that conveyed his earnest plea for freedom.

Gage swallowed hard against the emotion clogging his throat. He couldn't let this little boy be abandoned again.

"C'mon, buddy. Let's get up." He strode to the crib and gently lifted Connor into his arms. He smelled like peach-scented soap, and damp wisps of hair were matted to his forehead. Did that mean he didn't have a fever anymore? The baby's wide blue eyes scanned Gage's face as if assessing the situation. Gage waited, holding his breath, and braced for a meltdown. Slowly, Connor's mouth morphed into a toothy smile.

Thank You. Gage offered a silent prayer of gratitude, then looked around the room. He'd managed to avoid changing Connor's diaper yesterday, but he needed to step up and make an effort today. Even though he didn't have a clue how to accomplish the task. While Connor babbled happily, Gage spotted a plastic package of diapers propped against the wall and a carton labeled Wipes with a picture of a smiling infant on the front. He grabbed both of those and carried Connor out to the living room.

Mrs. Tomlinson glanced up from the e-reader in her hands. "There's our precious boy. Did you have a good nap?"

Connor grinned some more and clapped his hands together.

"Oh, you must be feeling better." Mrs. Tomlinson looked relieved. "Maybe his fever is gone."

"I hope so. As soon as his diaper is changed, I'll take

his temperature." Gage sank awkwardly to the floor and set Connor beside him. "Would you mind giving me some tips here?"

"Excuse me?"

"The diaper. Changing it. I—I have no idea how to do that."

"Oh. Right." Mrs. Tomlinson patted the sofa cushion beside her. "If you bring him to me, I can probably take care of it."

"No, no. I need to learn." Gage felt his cheeks redden. Incompetency made him feel weak. He hated that.

"All right. Start by laying him down on his back. Maybe give him a small toy to keep him occupied."

A few minutes later, after a lot of trial and error—and very little cooperation on Connor's part—Gage managed to change the diaper. He was in the process of snapping the bazillion snaps on the legs of Connor's one-piece outfit when boots thumped up the steps outside and then the front door flew open.

Skye came in, her cheeks flushed and her eyes wide with panic. "Oh, I'm so glad you're all okay."

"Skye, you scared me to death." Mrs. Tomlinson pressed her hand to her chest. "What are you doing home so early?"

Her icy gaze toggled from Connor to Gage. "Why didn't you answer my texts?"

Whoa. Gage sat back on his heels. Was she serious?

"Been a little busy." Gage gritted his teeth and helped Connor sit up. "Can I throw this diaper in the trash can or should I carry it outside?"

"The trash can under the kitchen sink is fine," Mrs. Tomlinson said. "Thank you."

He strode toward the kitchen, slowly counting down until Skye trotted after him. *Three, two, one.*

Sure enough, boots *tap-tap-tapped* behind him. "I need you to answer me when I text you. I was extremely worried when I didn't hear from you. My mom could've been hurt, or something might've happened to Connor. What am I supposed to think when you don't respond?"

Gage paused, one hand on the cabinet doorknob, adrenaline coursing through him. "That I'm handling it."

"It doesn't seem like you're handling things well when you can't find the time to send a brief text."

He threw the diaper in the trash, then straightened to his full height. In her navy wool peacoat belted at her slim waist, knee-high brown boots and windblown hair cascading around her shoulders, he had to admit she was stunning. Even if she was angry with him. Yet he couldn't ignore her attitude or the way her thoughtless words made him feel so unappreciated.

"You're going to have to learn to trust me, Skye."

Her face puckered, and she propped her hands on her hips.

"I understand that you have a lot on your mind. But if I don't answer you immediately, it means I'm most likely doing what I said I would—taking care of Connor or helping your mom."

"But neither one of you answered me. My mom is recovering from surgery, and Connor had a fever last night. I assumed the worst."

"The worst about who?" He'd struck a nerve. He could tell by the way she visibly flinched. "Now that you're here, I think I'll go. I've got an exam to study for."

"I didn't mean that the way it sounded. I—"

Really? He arched an eyebrow in disbelief, then moved past her into the living room and gave Connor's head a gentle pat on his way to the door. "See you next time, little dude."

"Gage, wait." Mrs. Tomlinson rose from the sofa and reached for her walker. "Please don't leave when you're angry."

"I'm not angry." Okay, maybe he was a little angry. He calmly shrugged into his jacket, then forced a polite smile. "If you don't think this arrangement is going to work out, just let me know, but I still plan to be involved in Connor's life—one way or another."

Without another word, he stepped outside and closed the door firmly behind him. That wasn't his proudest moment—leaving with a thinly veiled threat—but she'd come at him with her frustration and her doubt in his abilities, and he'd lost his cool. Despite their fight just now, he and Skye both shared a common objective— doing what was best for Connor. But now that Mrs. Tomlinson had revealed Skye didn't want to be a mother, how would she react when she found out about Ryan's parents?

Chapter Seven

"**D**id you apologize to Gage yet?" her mom asked, sitting at the table and calmly sipping her morning coffee.

Skye winced. Mom's simple question only amplified her guilt. "Not yet."

"You'd better."

Skye bit her lip and tucked a plastic bag full of carrot sticks into the thermal lunch tote and zipped it shut. Connor was down for his morning nap already. If she hurried, she could still get to the furniture store in time to open by ten.

"What if he doesn't show up to help this afternoon?"

"He will." Skye turned in a slow circle, looking for her keys.

"How do you know? He seemed upset when he left yesterday."

Skye located her keys under a pile of mail on the kitchen counter and turned to face Mom. "I'll call him when I get to the store."

"Promise?" Her mother shot her a doubtful look over the rim of her coffee cup.

"I promise." Skye rounded the table and gave her mom a quick peck on the cheek. "Aunt Linda will be here at ten fifteen to stay with you and Connor. She needs to leave after lunch."

"All the more reason for you to call and confirm that Gage is still coming." Mom flashed an innocent smile.

"You're relentless, you know that?"

"I'm only trying to help."

And maybe fix her up. Skye slid her feet into her boots. "I'll be back tonight. Call me if you need anything."

"Have a good day, sweetie," Mom called after her. "Don't forget to call Gage."

Skye chuckled as she put on her coat and grabbed her lunch bag and purse. The crisp winter air nipped at her cheeks as she stepped outside.

McKenna, where are you?

Skye had texted her a picture a few days ago of Connor smashing his fist into his birthday cake. Maybe it was a passive-aggressive move, sending her that photo, but she wanted McKenna to know what she was missing.

Still no response. Didn't McKenna care about her son? Since she'd intentionally left Connor behind and never mentioned when she'd be back, Skye was starting to question her cousin's motives. Checking in with Drew again hadn't helped, either. The missing person's report hadn't generated any leads at the sheriff's department. Was McKenna just ignoring Skye's attempts to reach out, or had something terrible happened to her?

Skye heaved a sigh and trudged through the snow to her car. McKenna's silence aside, she owed Gage an apology for the way she'd treated him. She cringed as she mentally replayed her snide words and subtle accusations, especially after he'd gone out of his way to be helpful. Why did she jump to conclusions so quickly?

A small part of her—the part that hated to admit she'd been wrong—hoped he wouldn't answer when she called. Mom was right, though. If he was so angry that he didn't want to help with Connor this afternoon—or any afternoon ever again—she needed to know.

Her stomach twisted at the thought of having zero child care options. Again. Aunt Linda graciously offered to step in on an as-needed basis, and a handful of other friends had done the same, but soon she'd run out of favors to call in. She needed consistent, reliable child care—not only for her own peace of mind, but because that was what Connor needed, as well.

After putting on her gloves, she scraped the snow and ice from her windshield and gave the engine a few extra minutes to warm up. By the time she finished and slid behind the wheel, shivering, the clock on her dash indicated she only had seven minutes to get to the store. Calling Gage would have to wait.

On the drive to work, she abandoned her usual morning radio show and rehearsed a hypothetical apology. "I'm sorry I was rude."

Not sincere enough. She cleared her throat. "I'm sorry I d-doubted you."

Better. No stuttering, though. "I'm sorry I didn't tru—"

Trust you. I'm sorry I didn't trust you.

The words died on her lips. How in the world would she manage to apologize if she couldn't even verbalize it while driving alone? She sighed and shook her head. Trust. Why was it so hard for her to conquer her fears?

She tightened her grip on the steering wheel and eased to a stop at one of the few traffic lights in Merritt's Crossing. The owner of the hardware store was neatly stacking shovels for sale in front of the entrance, while the young woman who just opened the new flower shop on the opposite corner was arranging a spring-themed display in her front window. She glanced up and waved at Skye.

Skye waved back, smiling at the stark contrast between her fellow business owners. With the whole town still looking like a winter wonderland, it was hard to imagine spring was supposedly just six weeks away. It was even harder to imagine that a flower shop might thrive in Merritt's Crossing, but the wind energy group brought new jobs and more families to town than ever before. It wasn't the sleepy little wheat-farming town just off the interstate anymore.

Could she stay here beyond Easter—manage the store and care for Connor?

A fresh wave of uncertainty washed over her. Before the idea grew legs, her phone rang. The light turned green and she cast a longing glance at her bag on the passenger seat. Not good to fumble for her phone and drive. Reluctantly, she accelerated through the intersection and down the street to the furniture store's parking lot.

By the time she found her phone in the depths of her purse, the call had gone to voice mail. She checked the ID. Her boss in Denver.

Her scalp prickled. Why was he calling? She still had six weeks of leave and one of her coworkers was covering her sales territory.

Skye tapped the screen and listened to the message.

"Hi, Skye. It's Jim. I'm sorry to bother you while you're on leave. Just wanted to let you know there's an unexpected opening in our division. One of your colleagues resigned yesterday, and I think you'd be a great fit for the role. It would be a promotion, of course, with a larger territory. Please call me when you have a few minutes. I hope your mom's recovery is going well. Take care."

A great fit for the role. He wouldn't have called if his offer wasn't genuine. She'd worked hard to hit sales targets and even earned a bonus last year. A promotion was one of her goals. And now it seemed so close, yet life was working against her.

Jim's offer came with a downside, though. The long hours, a new territory to cover, more responsibilities— not to mention more upheaval in Connor's life. He couldn't handle that. They didn't know what was going on with McKenna, and there was no way she'd dump the responsibility of Connor's care on Mom. With each passing day, she'd grown attached to the little boy, and despite her rude behavior yesterday, her attraction to Gage had grown, as well.

She couldn't ignore Connor's obvious affection for Gage, either. When he'd intentionally reached for Gage at the birthday party, and when Mom reported that Gage and Connor had a great first afternoon together, something inside her shifted. While she valued her independence and loved her work, if McKenna didn't come back for Connor, Skye's future plans couldn't just be about what she wanted.

Connor needed a stable home, and ideally, one that included a father, too. Maybe he would be better off with someone else, someone who was already married and could provide a stable home with two parents. She closed her eyes and rested her head on the steering wheel. While full-time day care was still a viable option, how could she seriously consider going back to Denver if it meant depriving Connor of a meaningful relationship with Gage?

* * *

He couldn't put it off another day—he had to tell Skye about Gerald and Irene's email. Waiting only made it harder and introduced the possibility that she'd think he was scheming behind her back. That was the last thing he needed.

Gage turned off his truck's ignition and stared at the double doors fronting Tomlinson's Furniture. If he spoke to Skye now, he'd still have time to squeeze in some studying for his exam before he went by her mom's house to take care of Connor.

He climbed out of the truck, hunched his shoulders against the bitter wind swirling down Main Street and strode toward the store's entrance. The living room furniture staged in the front window showcased an appealing inventory. A dark leather sofa, modern lamps, paired with nice end tables, and a large vase of fresh flowers invited customers to step inside.

The aroma of leather and upholstery mixed with citrus wafted toward him when he opened the door. An impressive arrangement of chairs, sofas and timeless wood furniture filled the showroom. Brick walls and vaulted ceilings with exposed pipes hinted at the building's age, while modern accessories indicated a store owner who kept up with current trends.

"Welcome to Tomlinson's. I'll be right with you," Skye called out from across the room without making eye contact. Two young women stood beside her in front of a bedroom set.

Gage nodded and shoved his hands in his jacket pockets, nervously shifting his weight from one leg to the other. A dark mahogany desk with a matching set of shelves sat against the wall to his right. An oval container shooting mist into the air explained the fruit-infused aroma, and several framed photographs mounted on the wall nearby caught his attention.

A black-and-white photo of the building from another era was surrounded by more framed color photos of a man and woman smiling proudly under the Tomlinson's sign, flanked by two boys and a gangly preteen girl. He grinned. Skye and her family—he recognized her blue eyes.

Footsteps clicked across the hardwood behind him, and he turned around.

"Gage?" Skye approached, her smile tentative, and Gage couldn't ignore the subtle *blip-blip-blip* of his pulse accelerating. "What brings you by?"

"I—I need to talk to you."

"I'm sorry about yesterday." She glanced down and fiddled with the hem of her pink-and-navy-plaid button-down shirt. When she met his gaze again, her expression was tinged with regret. "I shouldn't have jumped to conclusions and assumed the worst. I'm sorry I didn't… trust you."

Wow. Wasn't expecting that. He opened his mouth to respond, but no words came out.

"My family and I really appreciate you stepping in and helping us with Connor."

His mouth went dry. Oh no. That sounded like the beginning of a dismissal. "I—"

She held up her palm. "Please let me finish. I hope my rude behavior didn't run you off."

"I'm not here to bail, if that's what you're thinking."

Her mouth curved into a relieved smile. "I was so afraid you'd refuse to come back after the way I treated you."

"You can't get rid of me that easy." He pulled a small plastic bag from his jacket pocket. "Your mom said Connor ran out of medicine, so I stopped at the drugstore and picked up another bottle, so you'll have some on hand for next time. I hope I bought the right thing."

"That was nice of you." She took the bag and pulled out the tiny box of fever-reducing drops. "This is perfect. Thank you."

Her genuine smile sent a jolt of electricity arcing through him. He quickly squelched those sensations with logic. Once he told her about Gerald and Irene's email, she wouldn't be happy with the news. Ryan's parents expressing an interest in Connor totally threw a wrench into her well-ordered plans.

Unless she wanted to find a more permanent home for Connor. In that case, Ryan's parents might be the solution to her long-term problems.

Her brow furrowed. "Are you all right?"

"There's something else I need to tell you," he said.

"Oh?" She glanced over her shoulder. "I guess I can talk for a couple more minutes."

"It won't take long." Her customers were out of earshot on the other side of the showroom, circling the bedroom set. He took a deep breath. "I received an email from Ryan's parents this week. They just found out about Connor and contacted me for more information."

Eyes wide, she pressed her fingertips to her lips.

"I wrote back and confirmed Connor was Ryan's son and that he's living with family. Since I'm not Connor's guardian, I didn't think it was my place to tell them exactly what was going on."

"But you're their son's best friend. They trust you, I'm sure, and deserve to know the truth." She wrapped her arms around her torso. "I can't imagine how they must be feeling."

The tension in his shoulders loosened at the realization she wasn't going to panic over this news. "I've never asked you about survivor benefits because it's none of my business, but Ryan's parents are going to want to know. Are you aware if Connor received anything from the navy after Ryan passed?"

Skye shook her head. "McKenna never mentioned a word about it."

"So it's possible she has access to the money?" Gage's stomach clenched. "That might not be a good thing."

She rubbed her forehead with her fingertips. "No, probably not a good thing, given her track record."

"Gerald and Irene seem like solid, upstanding people. I doubt they're looking for money, but they will want to know all about Connor. Maybe even be involved in his life. Are you okay with that?"

Pain flashed in her eyes. She hesitated, then lifted one shoulder in a helpless shrug. "I—I don't know. Do they live close by? Are they asking for visitation?"

Her customers strode toward them. Gage pulled his keys from his pocket. "You have customers. We can talk more later. I'll be at your house at one o'clock like we planned, all right?"

"Thank you." Sadness lingered in her expression. "For everything."

He turned to leave, rubbing his knuckles against the hollow ache in his chest. He'd told her the truth, but it made him feel worse. Was it wrong that he wasn't okay with Gerald and Irene getting involved? Not that he didn't believe they had Connor's best interests in mind, but what if that meant Connor moved to Illinois with his grandparents? If Gage was honest, he hoped for more than just infrequent visits and the occasional photo of Connor. And he definitely wanted to spend more time with Skye, but without Connor, how was that possible?

Chapter Eight

It was standing room only around the air hockey table at Pizza Etc. on Saturday night. From her perch on a tall chair at the three-top table Skye had managed to score, she surveyed the crowded restaurant. Most of Merritt's Crossing had turned out to wish Bethany and her husband well on their new life in Arizona.

The server set a platter heaped with loaded nachos in the center of the table, along with a stack of napkins. "There you go, ladies," she said. "Can I get you anything else?"

"I think we're all set for now." Skye smiled at her. "Thank you."

"This looks amazing." Laramie reached for a napkin. "I'm not even going to think about how many calories are involved."

"Thank you for putting this party together," Bethany said. "Allen and I are really going to miss you guys."

"We're going to miss, too." Skye patted Bethany's arm. "This is all happening so quickly."

"I know." Bethany filled her plate with some nachos. "I can't tell you how sorry I am to leave you in a pinch with Connor. Have you found anyone else to help out?"

"Has she ever." Laramie waggled her eyebrows.

Skye rolled her eyes and reached for her diet soda. "Gage Westbrook is staying with Connor and Mom in the afternoon while I'm at the store. He's new in town and was a friend of Connor's dad. Just temporarily until I can find someone more permanent."

"It doesn't have to be temporary. I think he might be a keeper." Laramie's knowing grin made Skye chomp down on a mouthful of ice to keep from saying something snarky.

"Do you know if he's single?" Bethany asked.

"Not a clue," Skye mumbled around an ice cube. From the corner of her eye, she noted Gage lingering near the air hockey table, talking to one of Dane's friends. Again, the invisible thread tugged at her, heightening her awareness of his presence in the room.

Bethany used a napkin to mop up a glob of cheese on the table. "He might have a girlfriend we haven't met yet."

Skye's stomach lurched.

"Oh, you don't like that idea one bit, do you?" Laramie's triumphant grin made Skye wrinkle her nose in disgust. Sometimes knowing a person for more than a decade had its drawbacks. She never could hide anything from her best friend.

"If he has a girlfriend, she would not be happy to hear about you," Laramie said.

"Why not?" Skye glanced from Laramie to Bethany. How did this conversation even get started? Weren't they supposed to be talking about Bethany's new house in Arizona or something? "We're just friends."

"Right." Laramie's eyes glittered with mischief as she plucked another chip off the pile. "Friends who spend a lot of time taking care of a baby together."

"When Allen and I were first dating, he rented a garage apartment from Mrs. Gaither. Remember?" Bethany nudged Laramie's arm. "Out by the old Hartnett farm?"

"Oh yeah. Her gorgeous granddaughter moved in with her." Laramie nodded. "You were beside yourself."

"Thanks for the painful reminder." Bethany shot her a playful look. "Allen and I almost broke up over that."

"What does that have to do with Gage babysitting Connor?" Skye couldn't keep the irritation from her voice. "You guys are happily married now."

"Exactly." Laramie fired another knowing glance across their small table. "Bethany is trying to tell you that if Gage has a girlfriend, she wouldn't be happy about how much time he spends at your house, taking care of an adorable baby that isn't even his."

"Especially if she has long-term plans for the relationship," Bethany chimed in. "Just sayin'."

"Whoever this hypothetical girl is, she has nothing to worry about." Skye slid her drink aside and loaded a pile of nachos onto her own plate.

"Then why does he keep looking over here?" Laramie asked.

"What?" Skye froze, a chip coated in melted cheese and topped with black olives, jalapeños and tomatoes halfway to her mouth.

Bethany scanned the room. "He is looking over here quite a bit."

"Stop," Skye said. "Maybe he likes Laramie."

Bethany's grin stretched wide. "Then he'll have to arm wrestle your brother Jack to get to her."

Laramie's cheeks flushed, and she stared into her soda. "I don't think Jack has the nerve to speak to me."

Skye munched on her appetizer, caught in the awkward position of wanting Laramie to be happy, while acknowledging that Jack didn't seem courageous enough to offer more than polite conversation. "He did make an effort with his appearance at Connor's birthday party. Mom commented later that was the happiest she'd seen Jack since—in a long time."

She stopped short of mentioning her father's passing.

Laramie's smile wobbled. "He did look good."

Sidestepping that delicate topic, Bethany shifted the conversation back to Connor. "Connor is such a sweet little guy. I'm going to miss him, too. Will you let me know where he ends up?"

"Ends up?" Laramie's eyes widened. "What do you mean? Like foster care?"

"I'm sorry." Bethany grimaced. "Poor choice of words. Skye, you talk about Connor's situation as though it's temporary—until McKenna comes back. I assumed that was still the plan."

It was still the plan. Wasn't it? Skye wiped her greasy fingers on her napkin. "I'm still hoping she'll come back. Although we haven't heard anything from McKenna since she texted that she'd found some friends in Kansas. Gage did get an email from Connor's dad's parents, though. We're waiting to hear more about that."

"Where do they live?" Bethany asked.

"Not close by, I hope." Laramie frowned. "What if they want Connor to live with them?"

"I—I don't know what's going to happen." Skye squirmed in her chair. Laramie's line of questioning dredged up all kinds of worries. Not to mention her boss's voice mail making her question if she could balance caring for Connor with taking on a more demanding role at work. And allowing Gage to spend time with Connor had been hard enough. The thought of letting another stranger into Connor's world felt like a punch in the gut, but she couldn't keep pretending it wasn't a real possibility. Even if Ryan's parents appeared to be the best people on the planet, Connor wouldn't—

"When do you think you'll know more details?" Laramie's question pulled her back to the conversation.

"Gage and I talked about how to respond to the email today. It's only fair that Connor's grandparents know what's going on. After all, he's their only son's child. Gage let them know that Connor is living here in Colorado with extended family, and now we're waiting to hear more from them." She braved a quick glance across the room to where he still stood. He looked her way and caught her eye, then grinned. Warmth unfurled in her abdomen and she quickly looked away.

"Just friends, huh?" Laramie lifted an eyebrow. "I don't believe you."

With a flick of his wrist, Dane sent the white plastic disk spinning past Gage's lagging defense, scoring another goal in the impromptu Saturday-night air hockey tournament. A wave of approval rippled through the crowd milling around the air hockey table at Pizza Etc.

Gage gritted his teeth. Dane was ahead 7–6. How had he allowed himself to get roped into this?

"C'mon, Westbrook. Show me watcha got," Dane gloated, high-fiving one of his buddies standing near him at the other end of the table.

Should've stayed home and studied for his next exam.

Leaning over, Gage fished the puck out of the machine and stole a glance at the table nearby, where Skye sat with her friends. Supposedly, everyone was here to give Bethany and her husband—Dane's most recently defeated opponent—a proper send-off before they left for Arizona.

Right now, it felt more like a power move on Dane's part to maintain his title as unofficial air hockey champion. No wonder Drew had volunteered to stay with Connor and Mrs. T tonight.

"Quit stalling, man." Dane's face tightened with concentration.

"All right, all right." Gage set the puck on the smooth surface and smacked it against the left edge of the table, hoping it might ricochet into Dane's goal with sheer speed alone. Hoping that he might win the game and Skye might notice.

Dane smirked and blocked the shot effortlessly. "Why don't you challenge me a little?"

Gage bristled inside. Dane had been polite, friendly and professional during both orientation sessions. Gage had no reason to believe Dane's motivation was anything more than a drive to keep his winning streak alive. But the fierce look in his eyes, dogged determination to beat Gage as well as his appreciative comments about Skye when they were at the diner, made Gage suspect this might be something more.

He wanted to win this stupid game, too. If this was an unspoken turf war, he wasn't going down without a fight. Another volley sent the puck zinging back and forth between them, and Gage managed to defend his goal. He sneaked a glance at Skye to see if she was paying attention to this ridiculous showdown, then quickly sliced his paddle to deflect Dane's next shot.

"I see you looking at her," Dane scoffed. "How about winner asks her to dance?"

Gage's heart sped at the thought of holding Skye close. He fired another shot across the table.

"Yeah, you heard me. Winner asks her to dance."

The spectators ringing the table murmured to one another. Jack stood alone, just behind Dane, his expression unreadable. Gage hesitated. Skye wouldn't be happy if she found out about their competition.

"What's wrong?" Dane taunted. "Afraid I might win?"

He'd heard enough. There were plenty of women here they could both dance with, but if he didn't win and had to watch Dane dance with Skye—if she even said yes—he'd never hear the end of it.

"Deal." He flicked his paddle against the puck and it bounced off the right edge and sailed into Dane's goal unobstructed. Tied 7–7.

A fierce volley ensued, and the crowd around the table pressed in while the puck zipped back and forth. Gage was in the zone, blocking Dane's shots and firing back repeatedly. His arm ached from exertion, and a droplet of sweat trickled down his spine. Finally, he managed to slam one more shot across the table and it slid into Dane's goal for the win. Final score: 8–7.

"Congratulations." Dane tossed his paddle onto the table, then pushed through the crowd.

A smattering of applause broke out, but anxiety clenched Gage's stomach as he stared after him. He'd hate to do anything that might impact his local job prospects. Dane didn't have that kind of influence, though, did he? Besides, it was just a game.

"Don't worry about him." Jack clapped him on the shoulder. "He needs to lose every once in a while."

Gage offered a weak smile. "Yeah, probably."

"Here." Jack held up a quarter. "Go ask my sister to dance. I'll pick a nice slow song from the jukebox."

Gage sneaked a peek at Skye, who'd stood and put

on her jacket. "It looks like she's leaving. Let me offer to walk her to her car instead."

"Good plan." Jack pocketed his quarter. "Thanks for looking after my sister."

"You're welcome." Gage grabbed his jacket from a stool nearby and worked his way toward her, trying not to shove past anyone. He didn't want to seem too aggressive, yet he didn't want her to leave before he could at least offer to walk with her.

"Skye?" He gently pressed his hand against the sleeve of her jacket.

Laramie met his gaze, then exchanged a glance with Bethany as Skye turned to face him.

"Oh, hey." Surprise flashed in her eyes and her lips curved in a friendly smile. "How's it going?"

"Not bad. Just beat Dane in a game of air hockey." He couldn't help but brag a little, although he didn't mention that was the catalyst for crossing the restaurant to speak to her.

"Good for you." Skye shouldered her purse. "We were just getting ready to go. I promised Drew I'd be home by nine thirty."

"Mind if I walk you out?"

"I rode with Laramie, so—"

"That's all right," Laramie interrupted. "You can take her home, I don't mind."

Thank you. Gage owed her one. He studied Skye's expression, half expecting her to object.

"Oh." She hesitated. "I—I guess that would be fine."

"I'm ready when you are." He put on his jacket and waited while she said goodbye to her friends.

The crowd had shifted away from the air hockey game, and Jack or someone else must've dropped a quarter in the jukebox, because a familiar country song played, drawing several couples onto the black-and-white-checked linoleum floor. Gage let Skye lead the way to the front door, resisting the urge to press his hand to the small of her back and guide her.

Outside, the neon glow from the restaurant's sign cast a purple hue onto the sidewalk at their feet.

"I'm parked down the street. Hope you don't mind the walk." Gage's hand itched to reach for hers. Instead, he balled his fists in his jacket pockets. What was he thinking? Winning that game must've given him a shot of courage.

"I don't mind. The fresh air feels good."

The streetlights did little to detract from the stars dotting the inky black sky above. A group of ladies spilled out of a tavern nearby, their laughter puncturing the night air. Snow crunched beneath their boots as Skye walked beside him toward his truck.

He reached for the passenger door and opened it.

She hesitated and gazed up at him. "Thank you for driving me home."

The subtle curve of her smile drew his gaze to her lips. His mouth felt dry. "You're welcome."

Still she didn't move past him. They were inches apart now. His heart rate quickened as he searched her face, noticing not for the first time how her long thick eyelashes rimmed fathomless blue eyes.

Unable to resist any longer, his knuckles gently grazed her cheek as he dragged his thumb across the fullest part of her pink lower lip.

Her sharp intake of breath made him hesitate. She didn't back away, though.

"We probably shouldn't," she whispered as her hands twined around his neck.

"That doesn't feel like a no." He held back for an

excruciating instant, struggling to rein in his thoughts. She had her reasons for saying they shouldn't kiss, and he'd never force her.

"Kiss me." Her breath feathered his cheek as she went up on tiptoe and leaned into his embrace.

It was bold—asking him to kiss her. Skye knew it, yet she couldn't resist. As Gage's lips brushed hers, her defenses weakened further and she let herself get lost in the moment. He deepened the kiss while cupping her face gently in his hands. His aftershave or cologne or something, woodsy and crisp, enveloped her and teased her senses.

Wait! What are you thinking?

Her cautious nature battled with her senses, and for once she tried to ignore the voice of reason and savor Gage's mouth moving against hers.

What about Connor? Your life back in Denver?

She pushed her palms against his broad chest. "Stop. We have to stop."

His fingers skimmed the length of her jacket sleeves as she stepped back. Hurt flashed in his eyes. "Skye, what's wrong? What did I do?"

"Nothing." She bit her lip and looked away.

"Please. Talk to me. What happened?"

She shook her head. No. He'd only try to convince her that she was wrong. Just like her ex-boyfriend had twisted her words and made her question her logic, all because he wanted to control her.

"We shouldn't have kissed." Her voice wobbled, and she fought to keep her composure. Lifting her chin, she narrowed her gaze and forced herself to look him in the eye. "Please take me home."

"Okay." He waited while she got in his truck, then

closed the door. She pulled her phone from her purse and quickly texted Drew to let him know she was on her way.

Gage slid behind the wheel and put the key in the ignition, but didn't start the engine. The warmth of his gaze made her twist in her seat and stare out the passenger window.

"Skye, I would never do anything to hurt you. You know that, right?"

The tenderness in his words brought tears to her eyes. She dug her fingernails into her palms. "I said take me home."

Wordlessly, Gage started the truck and left the parking lot. A heavy silence filled the cab and she kept staring out into the darkness. She was an idiot. Succumbing to her selfish desires and completely losing focus on what really mattered. Connor. It might've been an amazing kiss, but it was a reckless choice, and it scared her to death. She couldn't risk being so vulnerable. Because vulnerability meant admitting she needed Gage. And the risk was too great and the pain still too raw from the last time she allowed herself to fall in love.

Chapter Nine

Why? Why had he kissed her?

Gage had asked himself that question a dozen times in the last three days and the answer hadn't changed— Skye was beautiful, they'd been alone under a star-filled sky and she'd asked him to.

Right? He'd certainly been caught up in the moment— her husky voice and slender fingers warm against the back of his neck had made him dizzy—but he hadn't imagined her request.

Connor interrupted his thoughts by handing him a blue-and-orange foam block decorated with pictures of animals and instruments, then clapped his hands awkwardly.

"Thanks, buddy. Nice clapping, by the way." Gage took the block and stacked it on top of the short tower he'd assembled in the middle of the living room floor. While the baby had napped for only an hour, Mrs. Tomlinson was still sleeping in her room after what she'd declared her toughest day at physical therapy yet. Gage didn't want to wake her. Connor squealed and kicked both feet with excitement, sending the blocks tumbling across the carpet. Instead of waiting for Gage to collect them and make a new stack, Connor got on all fours and crawled after a plastic airplane wedged under the love seat.

Gage quickly reached for his phone to record the activity. While Connor had crawled a little bit in the short time they'd spent together, Gage hadn't seen him move quite that quickly before. Skye and Mrs. Tomlinson would want to see the replay.

Skye had ignored all his efforts to interact in the three days since they'd kissed. His texts went unanswered, and she let both his calls go to voice mail. Maybe she'd respond to a cute video of Connor. While he filmed Connor in action, his thoughts cycled back to the kiss and he rehashed the whole encounter. As first kisses went, it was incredible, but he hated that he'd obviously done something to upset her.

Connor sat beside the love seat, sucking on one of the airplane's wings, so Gage stopped the video and quickly sent it to Skye, then put his phone away.

Dating hadn't been on his radar when he'd arrived in Merritt's Crossing. Finishing up his wind energy technician certification through the local community college and finding Connor were his priorities. Those objectives hadn't changed. His role in Connor's life turned into a much bigger blessing than he'd expected—and meeting Skye had made him revisit his previous failures in dating relationships. He hadn't had many healthy role models growing up. Dad left before Gage's third birthday, and when he had lived with his mom, she paraded an endless string of boyfriends in and out of their lives. His grandparents had stayed married, but Gage hadn't seen them often.

His chest tightened. Intimacy still scared him. Vulnerability seemed like a huge risk. Even with the mistakes the Tomlinson family admitted they'd made, Skye and her brothers and their mom still stuck together. He was in awe of their willingness to restructure their lives to meet Connor's needs, and still terrified about what it meant to be part of a family.

Maybe that was the problem. Skye sensed he was destined to be an outsider—a drifter—and she didn't trust him to stick around. Or maybe she thought he'd advocate for Ryan's parents to become Connor's legal guardians, which would only drive a wedge between them anyway. That certainly seemed more in line with her cautious, pragmatic nature. Whatever her reason for getting so upset, they needed to talk about it. Even if the kiss was a mistake, he couldn't leave things so unsettled. They needed to be able to work together for Connor's sake—especially when he told her about Gerald and Irene's plans.

Connor abandoned the airplane and crawled back toward Gage.

Gage had expected Skye to come home early from the store—barreling in the door and quizzing him about Connor's care. Instead, his afternoon shift had passed uneventfully, and his phone remained silent. Connor climbed into Gage's lap, then popped his thumb into his mouth. At least one person in this family trusted him.

"Want to read a book?"

Connor kicked one leg up and down repeatedly.

"I'll take that as a yes." Gage slid a stack of board books closer. "Let's see what we have here."

Resting his back against the love seat, Gage opened the book about race cars and counting to ten. As he turned the thick pages, he talked about each color and pointed out the numbers, enjoying the warmth of Connor's little body snuggled against his chest. Whatever happened in the future, he'd never forget these tender moments.

He was almost to the end of the book when a key turned in the lock and the front door opened. Skye came inside, her face drawn and smile tight.

Connor squealed and bounced up and down in Gage's lap.

"Hey, buddy." Skye's expression brightened a little, but she avoided eye contact with Gage.

His palms felt clammy and his mouth dry. "How was your day?"

"Good. Finally sold some furniture—a recliner." While she tugged off her boots and hung up her jacket, Connor chattered a string of nonsensical sounds. Gage had never been more grateful for the baby's ability to defuse the awkward tension.

"Where's Mom?" Skye padded toward them in her socks, then sank cross-legged on the floor. Connor wiggled and squirmed to get to her.

"She's taking a nap." Gage helped Connor off his lap so he could crawl to Skye.

"Look at you go." Skye held out her arms and Connor giggled as she scooped him up and pressed a juicy kiss to his cheek.

Gage looked away. Too bad she wasn't nearly as excited to see him. In her bright green sweater and dark blue jeans, gold hoop earrings and a hint of lip gloss on those kissable lips—meaningful conversation was the last thing on his mind. But her rejection stung, and he couldn't forget the look of regret he'd seen in her eyes. And they still had to talk—really talk—about their kiss and Ryan's parents' request.

"Do you have a few minutes?" He collected the

blocks and put them back in the toy bin. "There's something we need to discuss."

She ran her hand along the length of her ponytail, then flipped it over her shoulder and out of Connor's reach. Her cool, determined gaze lacked the spark he'd admired when she was in his arms. "If it's about our... If it's about Saturday night, then I think we can both agree it shouldn't have happened."

Oh. He rubbed his fingers along his jaw. So she still felt the kiss was a mistake? "We got caught up in the moment."

"Right."

Wrong. He wanted to argue, to distract Connor with a toy and pull her close for another kiss.

"We both know this is a temporary arrangement." She shifted Connor to her shoulder and patted him on the back gently with her palm while he sucked noisily on his fist.

"Absolutely." He despised anything temporary. It implied chaos and a lack of uncertainty—more scenarios that he despised. Sure, he didn't have a permanent job yet, although his advisor indicated Alta Vista would probably hire him. If not for a job in Merritt's Crossing, then for their new wind farm in Wyoming. Did she care if he left town?

Connor twisted in her arms and strained for the airplane he'd left on the floor earlier. His babbling escalated until she relented and set him on the floor beside her.

"I—I think it's best for all of us if we focus on Connor and try to be just friends." Her brow furrowed as she smoothed her hand across the top of Connor's head.

Just friends. The death spiral of all romantic relationships. Gage gritted his teeth. While he'd hoped the conversation might play out differently, he wasn't going to let her see she'd crushed his hopes. "You're right."

Oh, it about killed him to agree with her.

"It was just one kiss—hardly a commitment." Her casual words felt like another knife to his heart. It wasn't *just* a kiss. It was quite possibly the best first kiss of all first kisses. How could she dismiss it so easily?

"I'm genuinely sorry if I did anything that made you feel uncomfortable." Didn't he get credit for falling on the proverbial sword?

"I didn't feel coerced." Her tight smile returned, along with her impenetrable shield. Man, keeping him at arm's length was definitely her superpower.

"Good." He linked his arms across his chest. While he'd put off telling her about Ryan's parents because he thought it might hurt her, now he didn't care. If she morphed into all-business mode, then he'd do the same. All he wanted to do now was deliver the news and get out of there as quickly as possible.

He shot a quick glance at Connor, who'd reclaimed the airplane and sat nearby, sucking on the wing. "I need to let you know that Ryan's parents responded to my message. They'd like to visit as soon as possible."

Her porcelain skin went white and her chin dropped.

So maybe he could've eased into that announcement. "They live in Illinois, and as soon as I give them the go-ahead, they'll buy plane tickets."

Skye's Adam's apple bobbed as she swallowed hard. "H-how… I mean— When do you— How soon will they be here?"

His gut twisted. This hurt her more than he expected. "I imagine it depends on the price of tickets and if there are seats available. They have friends in Denver they can stay with, or I can offer to let them stay in my extra bedroom. You won't have to worry about hosting them or anything."

As if that somehow made the whole situation easier. The sheen of moisture in her eyes instantly made him regret he hadn't handled this differently.

"I'm not his legal guardian, so I can't stop them from seeing Connor, but… What does this mean?"

"It means they want to meet their only grandson." He palmed the back of his neck. "That's really all I know."

She glanced down and picked at her thumbnail. "Let me know when they're coming."

"Of course." His gaze traveled to Connor again, and a sickening sensation lodged in his core. What would happen when Gerald and Irene saw Connor? It wasn't like he and Skye had a future together. She'd made that abundantly clear just now. He wasn't prepared to take care of Connor by himself, not when he'd spend forty or more hours a week on a demanding, often-dangerous wind farm. Not that Skye would ever allow him to have custody anyway. So wasn't he doing the right thing by connecting Connor with his grandparents?

He had to get out of there. It hurt too much to think about where all this might lead. He pushed to his feet. "I'll keep you posted. See you tomorrow."

Cold air swirled around Skye as Gage closed the door, sending a shiver down her spine. Connor burst into tears and, honestly, she wanted to cry right along with him.

She turned around in time to see him crawl after Gage, then slap his palm against the closed door, sobbing.

Her vision blurred with fresh tears. Not only for Connor, but for the frigid conversation that created a seismic shift in her relationship with Gage. When she'd walked in a few minutes ago and saw Connor nestled in Gage's lap, reading a book, some rogue wave of domestic longing had crashed over her. With Gage in his faded jeans and gray sweatshirt that read Navy, a very attractive hint of stubble clinging to his jaw—it was a powerful image that offered a glimpse of a future she'd never imagined. Suddenly she was questioning her decision to never be a mom, and everything she'd rehearsed and planned to say about their kiss felt...wrong.

But she'd said it all anyway. Telling him the kiss was a mistake and holding fast to her boundaries didn't offer the satisfaction she'd hoped for. Instead she felt empty. Alone. This was what she wanted, right? Her independence, the career opportunities she deserved, freedom from a man who tried to diminish her dreams with his harsh words? Then why did she long to fling herself on the floor and mimic one of Connor's epic tantrums? She touched her fingers to her lips. Maybe because she couldn't forget how Gage's kiss made her feel. Safe. Cherished. Respected.

She stood and crossed to the foyer, then gently pulled Connor into her arms. "It's okay, buddy. He'll be back tomorrow."

Connor arched his back, resisting her attempts to comfort him. She carried him into the kitchen, hoping the suggestion of a snack might help, but he only wailed and pushed against her, trying to get free.

"Everything okay?"

Skye turned away from the pantry. Mom walked slowly toward them and stopped next to the dining room table, bracing her hands on the back of the chair. "He's mad because Gage left."

"I guess it's good he cries when the babysitter

leaves." Mom smiled. "That's how you know you've got a good one."

Skye ignored the comment and set Connor at her feet, then pulled out the bottom cabinet drawer. "Look. Lots of containers. Want to play?"

He shook his head and screamed until his face was dark red and tears tracked down his cheeks. Oh brother. Skye dragged the cuff of her sweater across her cheeks to staunch her own tears. Anxiety and frustration churned inside as she tried to think of a way to get Connor to stop crying.

"Are you all right, sweetheart?" Mom gingerly pulled out a chair and sat down.

"Let me help him first." Skye couldn't think straight, or tell her mom what was going on, when he was so upset. She poured Cheerios into a plastic bowl with a handle and slotted lid. "Connor, look." She knelt beside him and gently shook it to get his attention. "Would you like Cheerios?"

He drew a ragged breath, then cautiously stuck his chubby hand inside the container. It took him a minute to figure it out, but he eventually managed to get some cereal into his mouth.

"Very good." Skye praised him, and his toothy grin made her heart ache. Once his grandparents saw him, they wouldn't want to let him out of their sight.

What was she going to do?

Relieved he was occupied and mostly quiet, she joined her mother at the table.

"Tell me what happened." Mom's hand clasped hers.

"Gage says Ryan's parents want to see Connor. They're making arrangements to come from Illinois."

"Oh dear."

"I—I'm afraid they'll want to take him." Skye barely

choked out the words. "We aren't his legal guardians. If McKenna's not here, how will we stop them?"

"Let's not jump ahead." Mom's eyes glistened with tears. "This is all quite a shock, and I don't blame you for being upset."

Skye pulled her hand free and reached for a box of tissues. "There's more."

Mom's brow arched. "Go on."

"Gage and I, we, um, we kissed the other night. After Bethany and Allen's party."

"And that makes you cry?"

"I told him it shouldn't have happened." Shame crept over her. "I think that hurt his feelings."

Mom nodded. "I'm sure it did. Do you feel kissing him was a mistake?"

"The timing is all wrong. This—" She swept her hand in a circle. "What we're all doing for Connor feels temporary. What's going to happen when McKenna finally comes back, Gage gets a job offer and I go back to Denver?"

Her mother flinched.

Oh no. Skye's stomach plummeted. Mom thought she'd planned to stay? "Mom. You knew I was going back to Denver, right? That was our plan all along. I mean, I've already talked to my boss about this new promotion, and he says I'm one of the top candidates, so—"

"That was your plan," Mom interrupted, avoiding Skye's gaze as she picked at a loose thread in the quilted lavender place mat. "I guess I thought things were going so well you might change your mind."

"Going well?" Skye stared in disbelief. "Connor was kicked out of day care, we're relying on Aunt Linda and a stranger to help babysit, McKenna hasn't been heard from in weeks and the store—"

Whoa. Too much information. She clamped her mouth closed.

Mom's chin shot up, eyes wide. "What about the store?"

Skye's heart pounded.

"Skye." Mom's tone grew stern. "What's wrong with the store?"

Connor screeched, and Skye heard his palms slapping the linoleum as he crawled closer.

"I was going to wait until the end of the month to tell you." Skye's voice trembled.

"Tell me what?"

Connor grabbed Skye's leg and tried to stand, his little brow furrowed.

She couldn't move—paralyzed by the fear in Mom's eyes. "There isn't much money in your account, Mom. I—I don't know what Dad led you to believe, but you're not making enough to cover the utility bills."

Mom buried her face in her hands and started to sob. Connor grunted and pulled to a stand for the first time ever. Skye tried to smile at him through her blurred vision, and he began to cry, too.

They were a mess. A brokenhearted hot mess. She had no idea what to do about it, either.

Chapter Ten

Gage paced his apartment like a caged animal on Friday afternoon, anxiously awaiting Gerald and Irene's arrival. While he'd anticipated at least a week before their visit, they'd purchased tickets for the first available flight. He and Skye and her family had all of forty-eight hours to adjust to the announcement that they were coming for a weekend visit and expected to spend quality time with Connor.

Gage's stomach clenched. What if he couldn't meet their expectations? What if Connor refused to pay any attention to them? What if they announced more surprises, like further plans to be involved in Connor's life? The what-ifs were eating him alive.

It might've helped to talk with Skye about his concerns, but after his painful conversation with her about their never-should-have-happened kiss, he'd kept their interactions perfunctory. Polite. Respecting her boundaries was all he could do, because dwelling on their fleeting moment of happiness hurt too much. He wasn't the man for her, he reminded himself. It was best if he focused on keeping his word to Ryan and making sure Connor's needs were met.

He blew out a long breath and made a quick pass through the kitchen, stopping to move the vase of fresh flowers from the counter to the center of the table. Stepping back, he admired its new location. There. Irene seemed like a lady who'd appreciate a nice touch, and the woman who owned the new flower shop in town convinced him to go with the pink tulips.

Why are you trying so hard?

Regret. Fear. An intimidating mix of both. While the goal of the weekend focused on introducing them to Connor, he also anticipated a difficult conversation about Ryan's death. A shiver coursed down his spine. He didn't want to go there, either.

He continued down the hall for one last quick sweep of the guest room he'd hastily pulled together. Clearing out the last of the moving boxes, buying new sheets and a comforter, and making sure there were clean towels in the bathroom had kept him occupied the last two nights. Now the reality of hosting Ryan's parents for the weekend hit hard and part of him yearned to find an escape route. He'd mentioned a few motels and a historic bed-and-breakfast in the next town, but they'd declined. Spending time with Connor was their priority and they didn't want to waste time driving back and forth from a motel or their friends' house in Denver.

Lord, please don't let this be a huge mistake.

He breathed the earnest plea, knowing full well he'd let his guilt keep him from much more than superficial prayers lately. It was a heavy burden, yet he'd grown used to the weight of it. Would he ever break free? Was this weekend the first step toward freedom, or the makings of a more complicated scenario involving sweet, innocent Connor?

A firm knock at his door pulled him from his

thoughts. With his heart kicking against his ribs, he strode across his apartment and braced for seeing Gerald and Irene again.

"Hey." He offered what he hoped was a welcoming smile as he greeted them. "Come on in."

"Thank you." Gerald Simmons extended his hand. "Nice to see you again, Gage."

"You as well, sir." Gage shook his hand, noting the older man's firm grasp and immaculate purple cashmere sweater layered over a crisp purple checked button-down and wool slacks.

"Once a navy man, always a navy man, huh?" Mr. Simmons chuckled. "No need to call me sir."

"Hello, Mrs. Simmons." Gage stepped back to allow Ryan's parents in. "How was your flight?"

"Not too bad, I suppose. We don't typically fly coach, but on short notice, we had to make do." She patted her carefully styled short blond hair, even though it didn't look like a single strand would have the audacity to rebel. Her pearl earrings and leather handbag hinted at her taste for the finer things in life.

As she followed her husband into the apartment, Gage swallowed hard and closed the door. Ryan had rarely mentioned his parents' affluence—he wasn't one to boast about stuff like that. Their backgrounds hadn't really mattered as enlisted men anyway. Now, though, standing there with Mr. and Mrs. Simmons and without Ryan serving as a buffer, their differences stretched out like a canyon between them.

"Can I get you something to drink? Coffee? Water? Iced tea?" He smoothed his own hair self-consciously, grateful he'd taken the time to get it cut recently.

Mrs. Simmons's heels clicked on the laminate floor in the entryway, and her fingers fluttered to the buttons on her knee-length beige overcoat as her blue eyes surveyed his sparsely decorated living room. Suddenly he regretted inviting them to stay. This wasn't exactly the Ritz-Carlton. What would she think when she saw the guest room with no pictures on the walls and nothing but a single lamp on the nightstand?

"Nothing for me, thank you." Her smile was tight. "We'd prefer to see Connor as soon as possible."

Gage hesitated. Everything about her tone indicated she expected him to comply with her preferences. He glanced at the digital clock plugged in below his television.

"Connor's probably still napping, and they aren't expecting us until three thirty. Why don't I bring your bags in and give you a few minutes to get settled?"

An awkward silence filled the space between them.

"That sounds like a fantastic idea." Gerald's booming voice echoed off the walls and he clapped Gage's shoulder. "Irene, we'll be right back."

Her pencil-thin brows tented. "I suppose babies do nap, don't they? I'll wait here while you get the bags."

"We'll just be a minute." Gage stepped past her and grabbed his jacket and gloves from his closet. This weekend might be a challenge—for everyone. While he understood grief changed people, especially parents who'd lost their only child, Mrs. Simmons seemed noticeably uncomfortable and out of her element.

As he followed Gerald outside to their luxury rental car, Gage made a mental note to text Skye before he took Ryan's parents to the Tomlinsons' for the first time. If he had any hope of redeeming this situation, he had to drop a few hints. Mrs. Simmons's high expectations and abrasiveness required advance warning.

* * *

This was such a bad idea.

Skye trailed behind Connor as he crawled around the living room, casting toys aside and babbling to himself. She gathered the ones he discarded and tucked them back in the wicker basket beside the fireplace. It was a losing battle, trying to keep the house presentable for their guests. Why had she agreed to this meeting with Ryan's parents? Her empathy for their situation had morphed into dread once she found out they were coming. Gage's brief text message a few minutes ago had ratcheted her anxiety to a whole new level.

FYI... Our guests are a bit high-strung.

What did that even mean? The sound of a car pulling into the driveway sent her racing into the powder room in the hallway to check her reflection.

"Mom," she called out, "they're here."

Skye smoothed her hand down the front of her denim dress and quickly touched up her lipstick. Of all the things she'd done concerning Connor's care, she should've refused this request. McKenna wasn't even here—another major milestone and significant responsibility in the life of her son that she'd managed to avoid. It wasn't fair.

After their emergency family meeting last night, Drew had warned her this might lead to a custody battle. She didn't want to believe him but couldn't shake the ominous feeling looming over her like a storm rolling in off the Front Range. If there was a silver lining to these clouds, since she'd delivered the news that the store was in danger of going under, both her brothers had agreed to take shifts there, so she and Mom could visit with Ryan's parents.

Mom's deliberate footsteps in the hallway indicated she was making her way toward the living room.

"You look nice, sweetheart." Mom smiled from the bathroom doorway. "That dress with those short boots is so flattering."

"Thank you."

The doorbell rang, and Skye gently scooted past her mom. "I'll get it."

Thankfully, Mom had graduated from her walker to using a cane, and her pain had lessened. Skye was pleased to see she'd put on a new floral blouse, khaki pants and her nicest beige flats.

Her stomach churned as she picked Connor up and strode quickly to the door. She hesitated and pressed a quick kiss to his forehead. He squealed and grabbed a fistful of her hair.

"It's going to be okay. I promise," she whispered, more for her benefit than for his.

She opened the door and found Gage on the other side, standing beside an impeccably dressed older couple. Something indecipherable flashed in his eyes—regret? Empathy? It was gone before she could give it a second thought, replaced by a cautious smile.

"Hey." He reached out and gave Connor's leg a gentle squeeze. "How's it going?"

Connor immediately flung out his arms toward Gage and greeted him with an enthusiastic squeal.

"Hello." Skye strained to keep him from twisting out of her grasp, while forcing herself to welcome her guests. Not that it mattered, as they stood, transfixed, their eyes glued to the baby in her arms. "I'm Skye Tomlinson. You must be Mr. and Mrs. Simmons."

Mr. Simmons recovered his composure and cleared his throat. "Yes, yes. Hello, I'm Gerald. This is my wife, Irene."

Moisture glistened in Mrs. Simmons's eyes and her hand trembled as she grasped her husband's elbow.

"Please, come in." Skye moved back so they could all come inside. Connor's face puckered, and his mood threatened to shift. The longer she withheld him from Gage, the greater the risk of an epic meltdown. "Here." Panicked, she thrust him into Gage's arms. "Maybe it's better if you hold him."

"No problem." Gage grinned and gently swooped Connor into the air with a dramatic gasp. "Who wants to play airplane? This guy!"

Connor rewarded him with a belly laugh that softened the tension immediately.

Skye wanted to hug Gage but clasped her hands in front of her instead. "Mr. and Mrs. Simmons, I'd like for you to meet my mother, Rhonda Tomlinson."

Mom stepped forward and they exchanged pleasant greetings, although Mr. and Mrs. Simmons couldn't stop staring at Connor.

"He has Ryan's eyes, doesn't he?" Mrs. Simmons's smile wobbled as she glanced at her husband.

"Sure does." Mr. Simmons's voice was thick with emotion and he tracked Gage and Connor as they moved into the living room and closer to the toys.

"Please, make yourselves comfortable." Mom gestured toward the living room sofa. "Can we take your coats? Would you like some coffee or hot tea?"

"Hot tea sounds lovely." Mrs. Simmons slipped out of her wool overcoat and handed it to Skye. "Thank you."

Skye graciously took their coats and hung them up, trying not to think about how much Mrs. Simmons must've spent on her peach silk blouse and off-white linen trousers. The designer handbag she clutched probably wasn't a knockoff, either. Did McKenna know anything about Ryan's parents and their obvious wealth? Was she the one who reached out to them?

McKenna. Skye sighed. The girl had left a path of destruction wider than a tornado barreling across the High Plains. Maybe she wasn't coming back. And even if she did return, was she capable of being the mother Connor needed?

With her stomach in knots, Skye hurried into the kitchen, leaving Mom and Gage to handle the awkward small talk. Connor would undoubtedly remain the star of the show, at least until he threw a fit, giving her a few minutes to fix the tea. While she waited for the water in the electric kettle to boil, she arranged a tray of cookies Mom had somehow acquired and put cream and sugar in the china serving set reserved for special occasions.

She cringed. Why did she feel the need to impress Ryan's parents anyway? Was it her irrational compulsion to prove she was worthy of caring for Connor? That they hadn't messed him up in some way?

"Need any help?" Gage's deep voice pulled her from her thoughts.

She turned from the refrigerator to find him hovering at the end of the counter, hands tucked casually in his khaki pants pockets, while his presence seemed to fill the whole kitchen. The familiar scent of his woodsy aftershave wafted toward her, bombarding her with memories of their recent kiss. She immediately tamped those down. *Focus.*

"Where's Connor?"

His lips curved into a knowing smile, revealing a dimple she found hard to ignore. *Cue the butterflies.*

"I'm letting Irene hold him. Don't panic."

As predicted, her abdomen stirred with the unmistakable flitter she desperately longed to control. This wasn't the time to think about the mixture of warmth and amusement filling those hazel eyes of his, or the muscular curves of his upper arms, still quite evident even though he wore a moss green sweater. *Enough!*

She stubbornly tipped her chin. "I'm not panicking."

He arched a brow and held out his hands for the serving tray she'd loaded. "If you say so. Let me carry that for you."

Didn't he share her concerns about what Mr. and Mrs. Simmons might want? Or was this all part of his plan to make good on his promise to Ryan? She opened her mouth to ask him, but Connor burst into tears in the other room, and her heart rate sped as she brushed past Gage and rushed to Connor's rescue.

Gage carefully lowered the tray onto the table, then shot a quick glance over his shoulder. Mr. and Mrs. Simmons sat on the sofa, wearing stricken expressions, while Skye braced a distraught Connor against her shoulder, swaying gently to comfort him.

His breath caught as he discovered the trickle of blood oozing from Connor's mouth.

"Gage, can you get some paper towels or napkins, please?" Mrs. Tomlinson's voice remained calm, but the look in her eyes prompted him to act quickly.

Gage grabbed a handful of napkins from the holder in the middle of the table and crossed the room to Skye and Connor in quick strides.

"I—I don't know what happened." Mrs. Simmons splayed her hand across her chest, while her frantic gaze darted around the room. "One minute I was helping him stand at the coffee table, and the next, he was—"

"He can't stand up on his own yet." Skye's voice was harsh. Unforgiving.

"Here." Gage held a napkin gently to Connor's cheek. "Let's try to stop the bleeding."

"Bleeding?" Skye's eyes widened, and she shifted Connor into her arms for a better look. He wailed louder, the tears mixing with the blood staining his cheek.

"It's not as bad as it looks." Gage fought to keep his voice calm and cupped his other hand on top of Connor's head.

"This coffee table with these sharp edges really isn't a good idea." Mrs. Simmons's brow puckered. "He—"

"My late brother-in-law built that table." Mrs. Tomlinson raised her voice to be heard above the crying. "It's never been a problem before, and I raised three children in this house."

Oh boy. Gage clamped his jaw tight. *Here we go.* This was exactly the kind of conflict he'd hoped they'd avoid. He exchanged worried glances with Skye.

"Let's make sure the baby is okay, shall we?" Mr. Simmons stood and moved closer for a more thorough inspection, his weathered brow furrowed. "I've heard mouth injuries bleed more than other types."

Gage nodded. "I've heard that, too."

Connor tried to squirm away, but Gage firmly held the napkin against his gums.

"Shh, it's all right, sweetie," Skye murmured, awkwardly shifting him in her arms. "Let us help you."

"Why don't you sit down?" Mr. Simmons suggested. "It might help him relax a little, too."

Skye hesitated, then moved to the recliner in the corner. Gage followed, kneeling on the floor at her feet. A few minutes later, the bleeding had almost stopped, and Connor had calmed down, too.

Gage handed Connor a favorite plastic ball and attempted to examine his mouth. "I don't think he's missing any baby teeth, although to tell you the truth, I'm not sure how many he had."

"Me, either." Skye rested her cheek against the top of his head. "I'm just glad he's okay."

Gage's heart turned over. For a woman who didn't want to be a mother, she'd certainly reacted the way any mother would when a child was injured. He resisted the urge to give her arm a comforting squeeze and sat back on his heels instead.

"This is exactly why Gerald and I came as quickly as we could—to make sure our grandson was receiving proper care."

Gage felt Skye stiffen and heard her sharp intake of breath. He shot her a warning glance. *Wait.*

"Irene—"

"It needs to be said, Gerald." Mrs. Simmons's ramrod-straight posture and well-manicured hands clasped in her lap made Gage's scalp prickle. "After hearing about the child's mother and her issues, we are deeply troubled about his well-being."

"Excuse me?" Mrs. Tomlinson leaned forward. "What have you heard about Connor's mother?"

Gage's heart pounded. This time he didn't hesitate and reached over and twined his fingers with Skye's. Her skin felt cool to the touch. Much to his surprise, she held on tight.

"Tell them, Gerald." Mrs. Simmons angled her head

toward her husband. "Did you bring the letters and the photos?"

"What letters and photos?" Mrs. Tomlinson asked.

Mr. Simmons stood near the fireplace, hands clasped behind his back and his eyes downcast. "When we received Ryan's personal belongings from his apartment in Florida, there were a number of letters and pictures documenting his relationship with McKenna, which I did not bring along, but I'm more than willing to discuss what we've learned."

"Please do." Mrs. Tomlinson frowned, her knuckles white as she gripped her cane's handle.

"We spoke to Ryan's commanding officer once we saw the letters and pictures, and he was the one who revealed to us that Ryan had a child. That was difficult news for us to process, especially in the midst of our grief. We have a lot of questions and concerns, and in the last few months, we've pieced together a rather troubling picture of this young woman's history and…*lifestyle*." Mr. Simmons emphasized the last word, hinting at his disapproval. "While it isn't her fault Ryan never told us about her or the baby, the fact that she isn't here and has never reached out to us only confirms our deepest fears and cements our desire to make sure Connor is receiving proper care."

Gage's mind raced as he processed Mr. Simmons's statement as well as what he hadn't said. Was he implying that Connor was being neglected, and he and his wife intended to care for Connor permanently? Without thinking, he stroked his thumb over Skye's knuckles, hoping to offer at least a little comfort. He stole a glance from the corner of his eye. Her complexion was flushed, and she glared at Gerald.

"You still haven't mentioned your specific concerns

about McKenna. What issues are you referring to?" Skye asked.

Connor's babbling broke the tense silence.

"The email messages and photos she exchanged with our son indicated a lifestyle that revolved around partying, moving from place to place, an inability to hold a steady job. Nothing we've learned about her points to a woman who is able to be a mother."

"As you can imagine, it was extremely painful for us to find out about Connor this way." Mrs. Simmons's fingers glided over the strands of gold necklaces draped around her neck. "Then to learn his mother had abandoned him—I just couldn't rest until I saw for myself that he was all right."

"Despite what you might think about McKenna and my family—" Skye's voice was icy, direct "—I can assure you, we have made every effort to keep Connor safe, and to show him that he is loved."

Mrs. Simmons's thin smile was patronizing. "Have you?"

Whoa. Gage tightened his grip to keep Skye from coming unglued. If she lost her temper now, they'd have zero chance at a productive conversation. "Mrs. Simmons—"

"Perhaps we can all agree to pick this conversation up again tomorrow," Mr. Simmons suggested. "Thank you for your hospitality. I think we'd better give you all some space."

Relieved, Gage let go of Skye's hand and stood. "Mr. and Mrs. Simmons, why don't I take you to an early dinner?"

They all managed to exchange civil goodbyes, and Gage offered Skye one more apologetic glance before he slipped out the door. The shock and anger in her and her mother's faces knifed at him. He feared she'd never forgive him for engineering this meeting with Ryan's parents and Connor—especially if the situation escalated to an intense dispute over Connor's future.

Chapter Eleven

By Saturday evening, Skye was exhausted. Weary to the bone from dragging Connor all over creation, pretending to be a polite hostess for Mr. and Mrs. Simmons and still reeling from their obvious disapproval of her and her family.

Why was this happening? Hadn't she and her mother and brothers done everything in their power to make sure Connor was loved and cared for? While McKenna might not be fit for motherhood, didn't Mr. and Mrs. Simmons understand that taking him away from everything and everyone he knew was just as harmful?

In a corner booth at an upscale steak house more than an hour from home, Skye gritted her teeth and retrieved Connor's sippy cup after he'd flung it from his high chair. Mrs. Simmons insisted on one last meal together before they flew home in the morning.

"Maybe he's hungry." Mrs. Simmons glanced up from her menu, obviously quite proud of her ability to share her keen insights.

"Or tired. He's not used to skipping his nap." Skye tucked the cup in the diaper bag and handed him his pacifier instead. She wasn't in the mood for unsolicited advice, which Mrs. Simmons had doled out all day.

Satisfied, Connor sucked on it and banged his palms on the tabletop.

"Oh dear." Mrs. Simmons grimaced. "Those contraptions aren't ideal. Impacts his overbite. He should really learn to self-soothe."

"A baby who has lost both his parents should learn to self-soothe? I suppose you'd prefer he suck his thumb?" Skye forced a smile. "That contributes to a need for orthodontia later in life as well, and it's difficult to wean."

Gage nudged her leg with his own under the table. She nudged him back more forcefully. Seriously? He wanted her to behave after all they'd endured this weekend?

"What are you planning to order?" Mr. Simmons perused his menu, reading glasses perched on the end of his nose. "Skye, do you have a recommendation?"

She flipped her menu closed. "I'm having the vegetable soup and salad combo."

Gage shifted in his seat beside her. She sneaked a glance. Was he holding in a laugh? She didn't feel like steak and wasn't a fan of seafood and, frankly, didn't have much patience left. They'd insisted on the restaurant. Why did they need her input? Too bad Mom had bowed out gracefully and stayed home tonight— she'd be much better at defusing the tension blanketing their booth.

"Skye, I don't blame you for being protective, but I hope you know we want what's best for Connor, too." Mrs. Simmons's pinched expression morphed into one of sadness. "He is our only remaining connection to our son."

From the corner of her eye she saw Gage stiffen at the mention of Ryan. While she empathized with the older couple seated across from her, as well as with Gage and all they'd lost, she couldn't justify letting them have custody of a baby who'd already endured significant losses, too.

The waiter arrived to take their orders, saving her from articulating her thoughts. At least for now.

"Do you want to feed him while we wait for our meal?" Gage asked quietly. "I can go ask for some warm water to mix with the formula."

The knots in her shoulders loosened. He was trying to help make a difficult situation a tiny bit easier. "Please."

"I'll be back." Gage slid from the booth and worked his way toward the hostess at the front of the restaurant. Skye pulled out containers of prepared baby food, a bib and a plastic spoon from the diaper bag. It wasn't organic; she'd bought it at the grocery store, and Mrs. Simmons probably would have plenty to say about those choices, too.

"Have you always lived in Merritt's Crossing?" Mr. Simmons asked as she snapped the bib around Connor's neck.

"My parents have lived here their whole lives. I went to college in Fort Collins, then moved to Denver four years ago for a job in pharmaceutical sales."

"Oh, you must be eager to get back," Mrs. Simmons said.

Was she? Skye hesitated, then spooned pureed peaches into Connor's mouth. It was a slower pace here, and she had missed her friends at first. But she'd adjusted to her new routine, and Connor's sloppy kisses and contagious laughter made up for the exhaustion of meeting his needs. The notion of sticking around had crossed her mind for the first time today.

"I'm on leave until my mother fully recovers from knee surgery." Skye left her explanation at that. Honest, yet not oversharing. Who knew what sort of case they were assembling in their efforts to declare her family unfit to care for Connor.

A knot constricted her throat at the thought of him being whisked away to Chicago. They wouldn't do that, would they? Did Colorado law allow grandparents to cross state lines and demand visitation rights?

Gage returned and quickly fixed Connor's bottle.

Connor screeched as soon as he caught sight of it and pushed Skye's hand away, rejecting the rest of the baby food. The customers seated at the next booth fired disapproving glances their direction.

"How about if I give him the bottle?" Gage leaned close, his breath feathering against her cheek. She wanted to hug him but gave him a weak smile instead. How did he know she was on the verge of tears?

"Please." She maneuvered Connor out of his high chair and onto Gage's lap, then scooted over to make a little more room for the baby in their half of the booth. As Gage settled Connor in the crook of his arm and offered the bottle, another wave of longing crashed over her. Visions of dinner out with friends—instead of her new adversaries—or family meals shared with Mom and her brothers played in her head, all with Gage and Connor beside her.

"While the two of you make quite a pair, I'm sure it's no secret by now that we want custody of Connor." Mr. Simmons crossed his arms across his chest. "When we get back to Chicago, I'll have our attorney prepare the paperwork."

Like a needle to a balloon, his blunt words ruptured her domestic daydream. "Excuse me?"

"We're grateful for all you've done, taking time away from your career, but we don't expect you to rearrange your life to accommodate Connor's needs." Mrs. Simmons trotted out her patronizing smile again. "We have the resources at our fingertips to ensure he is well taken care of."

Sparks ignited in her vision. "What happens when one of you has a health crisis? Who will take care of him when you are no longer able?" Her voice rose an octave. "McKenna hasn't relinquished her parental rights. It's illegal for you to take Connor without her permission."

"Please, calm down." Mr. Simmons held up both palms. "We're not suggesting we take Connor with us now. However, your cousin might be easily persuaded to give up her rights if she knew what we were offering."

Skye wanted to throw up. "You'd bribe her? What court would allow that?"

A muscle in Mr. Simmons's jaw knotted. "No one said anything about a bribe."

"But that's what you meant, right?" Skye dug her fingernails into her palms to keep from pounding her fist on the table. "Tell me, how much would you pay her in exchange for her baby?"

"Skye." Gage's voice carried a warning, but she didn't care. Her body trembled as she leaned across the table.

"I'm sorry that you lost your son. Truly, I am, but taking Connor away from everything he's known isn't in his best interests."

"It is reasonable and prudent for us to have visitation rights," Mrs. Simmons said, her eyes flashing. "You can't keep him from us."

Skye heaved an exasperated breath. "Visitation and custody are not the same."

The waiter arrived with their meals, but Skye wasn't hungry anymore. While Gage attempted to eat, she held Connor and rocked him gently until he fell asleep with his head on her shoulder.

Mr. and Mrs. Simmons ate in silence. The hum of muffled conversation and silverware clinking against plates filtered around them, and Skye took deep breaths in an effort to calm down. She rested her cheek against Connor's head as he released a contented sigh.

They couldn't take him. Even if she exhausted all her resources, and it was an uphill battle, she'd fight to keep Connor with the only family he'd known.

Early the next morning, Gage helped Mr. Simmons load their luggage into the trunk of their rental car while Mrs. Simmons sat in the passenger seat. They'd spent the whole weekend either talking about Connor or arguing about his care, and never once mentioned Ryan. Gage's pulse sped. He was almost out of time.

"I'm sorry." He scraped his hand across his face as Mr. Simmons slammed the trunk lid closed.

"What for?"

"For everything. For not trying harder to save Ryan, for not helping you come to some sort of agreement with Skye and her family about Connor. I—"

"Listen." Mr. Simmons's blue eyes bored into Gage. "We might not agree on much, but I want you to hear me on this. You are not responsible for Ryan's death. Understand?"

"I'm afraid you're wrong, sir. If I had—"

"Son, I read the report until I had it memorized. Spoke to your former commanding officer and the senior enlisted officer numerous times. Human error, limited budget for our defense department and faulty equipment are responsible for Ryan's death. Not you."

No. Emotion clogged his throat. He should've gone back instead of thinking of himself first. If only he'd tried harder, there would've been enough time—

"I can tell you don't believe me." Mr. Simmons's breath left white puffs in the crisp morning air. "Maybe in time you'll be able to accept what I've said and finally forgive yourself. Irene and I certainly don't hold a grudge. The navy has taken appropriate disciplinary action for the men who messed up that night."

"Thank you, sir." Gage barely choked out the words.

"It's unfortunate that you're caught in the middle of this situation with our grandson." Mr. Simmons clapped Gage's shoulder one last time, then circled around to the driver's side. "I realize you don't have any skin in the game, and we appreciate you looking out for him anyway."

"I'm—"

"Thanks again. We'll be in touch." One last tight smile, an obligatory wave from Mrs. Simmons, and they drove away.

Gage stared after them in disbelief. *No skin in the game?* That wasn't true at all. He loved Connor, and he cared deeply about Skye. The realization stunned him—a one-two punch on the heels of Mr. Simmons's candid statements about Ryan's accident.

If only she cared about him. He'd managed to keep the peace at the restaurant last night, and everyone said goodbye on civil terms, but barely. Thankfully Skye and Connor had come separately, otherwise it might've been a very contentious drive to Merritt's Crossing.

He shook his head and strode back inside his apartment. She'd had trust issues before Ryan's parents visited. He could only imagine how she felt after the way they'd behaved. While he hadn't planned the visit, she no doubt blamed him for his role. Add that to the ever-growing list of reasons why she probably wasn't a fan of him.

The week ahead required more studying, completing online assignments and preparing for another climb at the wind farm on Friday. None of that held his attention, though—not with the memory of Skye's reaction at dinner last night still cycling through his brain. She was right. Bribing McKenna to give up Connor was wrong.

He went through the motions of cleaning up the breakfast dishes, his new reality weighing like an elephant on his chest. Maybe Mr. and Mrs. Simmons didn't blame him for Ryan's death, and the navy had ruled it an accident, but he kept circling back around to the fact that Connor's life was forever altered by the events of that day.

After throwing in a load of laundry, he dressed for church. On the way to Merritt's Crossing Community Church, he prayed and asked for guidance. Doubts threatened his confidence, though. The situation seemed impossible to resolve—at least the resolution he hoped for—he and Skye and Connor all together.

In the parking lot, he steered his truck into an empty space as Laramie climbed out of her car nearby and then lifted a baby from a car seat—Connor? He glanced around the parking lot. Where was Skye? He cut the engine and hurried to catch up.

"Laramie," he called after her. "Hang on."

She turned and smiled. Connor's eyes widened, and he opened and closed his fist in a clumsy wave.

Gage's steps faltered. "Nice waving, little dude."

"Hey, Gage." Laramie shifted Connor in her arms. "How's it going?"

"Not great." He palmed his neck. "Did Skye tell you about last night?"

"She did. Which is why I sent her for a short retreat."

"What do you mean? Where is she?"

"I'm taking care of Connor today, Drew is at home with Mrs. Tomlinson and we sent Skye to Denver."

"Oh." He tried not to let his disappointment show. It was great she was getting away to recharge, but he also wanted to see her. To make sure she was all right, and to talk about what might happen next.

"You didn't hear this from me, but her spa appointment is finished at three thirty." Laramie grinned. "I bet she wouldn't mind if you were waiting outside to take her to an early dinner."

He hesitated. "Are you sure she isn't sick of me?"

Connor babbled incessantly, drawing the attention of curious onlookers on their way into the church. What if Skye was angry that he surprised her? Maybe she wanted to be alone and as far away as possible from anything that reminded her of their emotionally draining weekend.

"One more teeny, tiny hint. There's a restaurant near Washington Park that she adores." Laramie fumbled for her phone. "I've made a reservation already. Give me a second, and I'll text you the addresses for the spa and the restaurant."

Gage swallowed hard. Dinner reservations. Picking her up at the spa. This had the potential to go off the rails if Skye wasn't pleased with him hijacking her plans. "If you're sure—"

"Trust me." Laramie gave him a playful shove. "Now, go."

"All right, all right." He jogged back to his truck, a

smile tugging at his lips. What was the worst that could happen? Skye wasn't shy about speaking her mind. If she didn't want to go to dinner, she'd make her feelings known. More than anything, he desperately wanted to redeem this weekend and prove to her that no matter what happened with Connor, he wanted to be with her.

Chapter Twelve

"Thank you so much." Skye smiled at the attendant behind the front desk at the spa. "Everything was wonderful."

"So glad you enjoyed it." The young woman handed her a receipt. "We hope to see you again soon."

"Me, too." Skye dropped the receipt in her purse and tried not to think about how much the massage and facial cost. It was well worth it. This was the most relaxed she'd felt since, well, since she'd gone to Merritt's Crossing. Her limbs felt loose and fluid, and the muscles between her shoulder blades weren't scrunched in tense knots anymore. She'd forgotten how good it felt to be pampered, if only for a short time.

She looped her scarf around her neck, shouldered her purse, then stepped outside. While snow still edged the sidewalks, the concrete was bare and the blue sky stretched overhead with hardly a cloud in sight. The midafternoon sunshine on her face offered a hint of warmth. Maybe spring wasn't far away after all.

As she rounded the corner of the building, her steps faltered at the sight of a familiar blue pickup parked nearby.

"Oh my." Her breath hitched. Gage leaned against the driver's side, one long denim-clad leg crossed over the other, with a bouquet of daffodils wrapped in brown paper in his arms. In his leather jacket and aviator sunglasses, his handsome features were more striking than ever.

"Hey." He straightened to his full height and removed his sunglasses. She strode closer, stopping in front of him.

"What are you doing here?"

"Can't a guy surprise a lady every once in a while?" He held out the flowers. "These are for you."

She took the bouquet, noting the way her pulse did a subtle *blip-blip-blip* as his fingers grazed hers. "Thank you. They're lovely."

"You're welcome."

"You didn't have to drive all the way to Denver to bring me flowers." She tilted her head to one side. "Didn't anyone tell you there's a new flower shop in Merritt's Crossing?"

"But you're not in Merritt's Crossing, so where's the fun in that?"

Her heart cartwheeled at his flirtatious banter.

"If you knew where to find me, were you a part of this covert operation to get me out of town?"

"I wish." He reached over and tucked a strand of hair behind her ear. "You deserve a break."

She shivered at his touch but didn't step back. His imposing presence didn't intimidate her like when they'd first met.

"If you're free, I'd love to take you to dinner. Laramie set us up with a reservation at one of your favorite places."

Skye smiled. Laramie. Her bold attempt at matchmaking was impressive. She glanced down at her yoga pants, T-shirt and ballet flats. "I'm not really dressed appropriately for dinner."

"That's debatable." He held her gaze. "I think you look wonderful."

Warmth heated her cheeks. "Thank you. I'd still rather change into something nicer than this."

"So that's a yes, then?" he asked, his expression hopeful.

"Yes."

"Good." He smiled. "I hope it's a better experience than our last visit to a nice restaurant."

Laughter bubbled up. "Me, too." She wrinkled her nose. "You don't think I was too childish?"

"Not at all." His eyes searched her face. "I thought you did a wonderful job speaking your mind. Connor's fortunate to have you in his corner."

Her heart hammered. She wanted to trust him. She really did. He hadn't given her any reason not to. He'd cared for Connor and helped Mom so selflessly. Inviting him to her apartment a few blocks away while she changed clothes was too forward, though.

"What's wrong? You look worried." He glanced down and dragged the toe of his boot against the snow-crusted parking lot. "I shouldn't have assumed you'd want to have dinner with me."

"It's—it's not that. I do want to have dinner with you." She met his cautious gaze. His expression looked guarded. Did he think she might blow him off? "I was trying to figure out the logistics, because parking can be a challenge. If I text you the address of a coffee shop in my neighborhood, will you meet me there in thirty minutes?"

"Are you sure?"

She nodded. "We can grab coffee and walk through the park before dinner."

His wide smile made warmth and excitement spread through her chest. This wasn't how she'd planned to spend the rest of her day. Did everything always have to be the way she wanted, though? Hadn't the last few months taught her there was good in embracing the unexpected? Maybe this spontaneous outing was worth the risk. Maybe *he* was worth the risk.

Gage sank into an overstuffed chair in the corner of a busy Denver coffee shop. He'd sensed Skye's discomfort at inviting him to follow her to her apartment and tried not to let it bother him. She was smart. Cautious. Accustomed to life in a midsize city. But he couldn't ignore the underlying current of uncertainty that sometimes resurfaced, flashing across her features before she quickly regained control. What had happened to her?

He dug his fingers into the armrests of his chair and tried not to think about what kind of a man might treat such a beautiful woman poorly. How could he convince her that he cared deeply and admired her strength and confidence?

The door opened, and he glanced up, hoping it was Skye. Instead, three young women strode in, all glued to their phones. A coffee grinder rumbled behind the counter, followed by the hiss of steam from the espresso machine. Gage surveyed the modern decor, people sitting at tables hunched over their laptops and the line of customers snaking from the register.

Outside, a steady stream of cars, pedestrians and even a few bike riders filled the city streets. This was quite a change from the slower pace of Merritt's Crossing. The buildings around the coffee shop looked like a mix of high-end condos and restored Victorian homes—the kind of place where young career-oriented single people might live to be close to the amenities and night-life of downtown, without giving up the vibe of a neighborhood.

Did Skye enjoy living here? She'd only committed to a short stay with her mom, and her leave from her job was probably coming to an end. What did that mean for Connor? For him? It seemed unlikely that Gerald and Irene would gain custody of Connor quickly, but if they did, might Skye resume her life here right where she'd left off?

All these questions only added to his unsettling discomfort. He shifted in his seat, bouncing his knee up and down, and stared out the window impatiently. When he caught a glimpse of Skye walking along the sidewalk in a floral-print dress, knee-high brown leather boots, with a coat draped over her arm and small purse dangling from her shoulder, his heart thrummed in his chest. Her long hair bounced across her shoulders as she walked, and he had to grit his teeth as two men passed her and offered appreciative glances.

Oblivious to them, she met Gage's eyes through the window and smiled. He stood and met her at the door.

"I'm sorry to keep you waiting," she said, joining him inside. "A friend is staying at my apartment while I'm away, and I felt rude rushing back out so quickly."

"No problem." Gage's shoulder brushed against hers as they took their places at the back of the line. "I'm a great people watcher."

"There's a lot to see compared to Merritt's Crossing."

Gage resisted the urge to ask which she preferred—Denver or Merritt's Crossing. He was afraid he might not like the answer.

A few minutes later, to-go cups in hand, they left the coffee shop.

"Feel like a walk?" Skye asked. "There's a nice trail around the lake a couple of blocks from here."

"Sounds good."

They walked in companionable silence, until his regrets from their visit with Ryan's parents threatened to steal all the joy of being alone with Skye. "I'm so sorry that our interaction with Gerald and Irene was contentious. I feel partly responsible for that."

She glanced up at him, eyes round. "Why?"

His mouth felt as dry as sandpaper as he forced the words out. "Helping Connor connect with his grandparents felt like a positive step in keeping my promise to Ryan. If I'd known what they'd propose once they got here, and what that would mean for you and your family, I—I would've given it more careful thought."

He stared at the lake coming into view and braced for Skye's reaction.

"I think you did what anyone in your situation would do—help two grieving people connect with their grandson."

The tightness in his chest loosened. "Really?"

Skye nodded. "I'm not thrilled about their strategy for being more involved in Connor's life, but I don't blame you for their actions or the things they said while they were here."

They walked in silence and then she glanced at him again. "If you don't mind my asking, why have you remained so loyal to Connor through all of this? Is it still just about keeping a promise to Ryan?"

"It's more…complicated." The anxiety of reliving those last horrifying moments sent a shiver down his spine. The darkness from the loss of power belowdecks, men scrambling to escape the damaged compartments, the acrid scent of smoke...

"The day Ryan died, we were at sea, after a long day of training exercises on our sub. I was getting ready to go to sleep, and Ryan was standing watch because we'd traded shifts. There was a horrible fire—"

His heart pounded in his chest. "I—I tried to get to Ryan's station, but the fire was spreading, and I didn't have time..." He trailed off, his throat clogged with emotion. "Ryan and five other guys didn't make it out. I've always blamed myself because I was the one who traded shifts with Ryan."

Skye gently squeezed his arm. They stopped walking, and she faced him. "I am so sorry. It must've been awful."

"Thank you." He looked away, wishing he hadn't forgotten his sunglasses in his truck. Letting her see his anguish scared him. "In the eyes of the navy and even according to Gerald and Irene, the accident was blamed on human error and equipment failure, due to budget shortfalls, but I can't help thinking that maybe if I'd tried harder, acted a split second sooner, Ryan might still be here. If I hadn't asked Ryan to trade shifts with me, Connor would have a dad."

"Look at me." Her voice was tender, and the comfort of her fingers still wrapped around his forearm drew his gaze to meet hers. "You can't keep carrying the weight of that guilt. It's going to eat you up inside. Like you said, the cause was equipment failure, so how could you have prevented that?"

He searched her face. She was right; he couldn't. Yet he didn't know how to surrender it, either. "It's not that simple."

Empathy filled her eyes. "I know," she whispered.

They stood there staring at one another, unspoken words lingering in the space between them. His arms ached to pull her against him, to ask her to share the burden she carried yet kept buried deep, as well. Instead, her hand dropped to her side, he tore his gaze away and they resumed their walk. He wouldn't force her to share, because he was afraid she'd retreat and never allow herself to be vulnerable.

Gage blamed himself. It all made sense now—his quest to find McKenna and Connor, his unwavering determination to be a part of Connor's life and his selfless care of the baby. Skye's heart swelled. She knew what it was like to carry blame like that. If she'd made better choices, maybe she wouldn't bear the emotional scars of a controlling boyfriend. If her family hadn't enabled McKenna or let the feud between Dad and Uncle Kenny fester, life might've turned out differently for her cousin. Connor, too.

"What are you thinking about?" Gage gently nudged her elbow as they left the city streets and strode down the paved path circling the lake.

The first signs of spring dotted the ground between them and the water. New daffodils and crocuses poked up, and patches of grass had emerged in places where the sun had melted away the snow. Could these symbols of spring and renewal signal a change in her own life, too?

She sighed. "Thinking about McKenna and the past and if we will ever break free from the stuff that weighs us down. What's going to happen to Connor."

Gage chucked his coffee cup in a trash can. "If you don't mind my asking, what's weighing you down?"

She stared across the lake. A breeze rippled the blue-gray water, and a shiver raced down her spine.

Gage's arm looped around her shoulders. "Are you cold?"

The concern in his voice and the warmth of his gaze cracked something open inside, and she let herself lean into him. "Scared."

They stopped walking and he gestured to a wood-and-wrought-iron bench facing the water. "Want to sit for a few minutes?"

She nodded. Once they sat down, she set her half-finished coffee and her purse beside her, then draped her coat around her shoulders. Gage rested his arm across the back of the bench without touching her. She wanted to lean into him again but settled for her leg barely resting against his. The warmth of the sun at their backs would have to be enough.

"Is this okay?"

Her mouth was as dry as cotton and blood rushed behind her ears. Gage waited patiently, his concerned gaze trained on her. The words piled up in her head, like cars on the freeway during rush hour. Where to begin? It wasn't easy to share her story, which was probably why she hadn't told anyone other than Laramie and her therapist. "I— The guy I dated a couple years ago, he wasn't very good to me."

"What happened?"

"At first, everything seemed fine. Great, actually. He was kind and funny and very much a gentleman. There were gifts delivered to my apartment, and he took me to some of the best restaurants—" She glanced down and picked at a loose thread on the cuff of her sleeve. "I should've seen the signs. Maybe I didn't want to."

"What kind of signs?"

"He had a temper and an intense competitive streak. Most of the time it was directed at other people—sports, a competitor in a video game, a heated political debate with a friend at dinner. Occasionally, he'd say something really harsh to me, especially if I'd had a productive week at work or earned a bonus or something."

"I really don't like where this is going," Gage said.

She plowed on, staring straight ahead. "One night we went back to my apartment after dinner out with friends, and I invited him in to watch the rest of a football game. I made one comment about an assistant coach's appearance—he was very handsome—and I should've kept my opinion to myself. My boyfriend came unglued."

Gage's fingers gently cupped her shoulder and he scooted closer. "I am so sorry."

Her stomach churned, and her fingers trembled as the memories came rushing back. "He was yelling and making demeaning comments about women." Still avoiding his gaze, she smoothed her hand over her skirt. "Most of the time, I can focus on the positive and ignore the memory of the horrible things he said. But I'll never forget the way he made me feel. Like I was nothing."

"Hey." Gage touched his fingertip to her chin and tenderly angled her face toward his. "You are a beautiful, intelligent woman with a generous heart and an unwavering inner strength. Don't let anyone tell you otherwise."

Her heart soared at his kind words. "Thank you," she whispered.

"You deserve to be treated well." His eyes had darkened, and they scanned her face, before landing on her mouth.

Her breath caught, and she quickly pushed to her

feet. "It's a beautiful day. Do you want to keep walking around the lake?"

Disappointment flashed in Gage's eyes before he pushed to his feet and joined her. "Sure."

She winced and turned away. Kissing Gage again now would only complicate matters. While she was determined to do what was best for Connor, she hadn't declined the promotion at work. It was still an option, as long as she found a day care with space available in Denver. If her time in Merritt's Crossing was coming to an end, she didn't want to mislead Gage. Between working full-time and caring for Connor and Gage starting his new job, they wouldn't have space in their busy lives for one another.

She stole a quick glance at him as they walked in silence. Her stomach twisted in knots. While she'd started thinking about staying in Merritt's Crossing permanently, spending the afternoon in Denver made her acutely aware of how difficult it would be to resign from her job and move back home. She'd have to tell him about her promotion. Soon.

After dinner, tucked away at a round table in an intimate corner of Skye's favorite bistro, Gage reached across the white tablecloth and took her hand. The fantastic food, including the cheesecake they'd just shared, and the flickering candlelight between them blotted out any doubts he might've had about their spontaneous outing. She smiled, and he felt his heart expand.

"I hate to ruin a perfect evening by talking about reality," he said. "But what do you think is going to happen with Connor?"

Her smile faltered. "I'm going to have to hire an

attorney. I want to become Connor's permanent legal guardian."

His stomach tightened. "Have you heard from McKenna?"

"I texted her and told her Ryan's parents had come to visit and demanded to see Connor. That got her attention because she finally answered me. She said she was sorry she hadn't been in touch, but she'd checked herself into rehab in Kansas City."

Rehab. Maybe Gerald and Irene weren't so wrong about her after all.

"Do you think she'll come home when she's finished?"

Skye shrugged. "She didn't say. I tried to get her to tell me more, but she ignored the rest of my messages."

"Wouldn't the threat of losing her child motivate her?"

"Maybe in her mind, she already lost him when she left." Skye frowned. "This must seem so ridiculous. You probably had a much different upbringing with a mom, a dad and a golden retriever in your fenced yard."

Her words caught him by surprise. Had he led her to believe that was the case? He scraped some crumbs from the table with his palm and carefully measured his response before he spoke.

"Gage?" She leaned closer. "Did I say something wrong?"

"My mom was a lot like McKenna," he said softly. "That's why I care so much about what happens to Connor—I don't want him to grow up like I did."

Her eyes widened. "I—I didn't know. I'm sorry. What I said sounds so insensitive now."

"It's all right. I didn't exactly advertise my past."

"But it's the driving force behind your concern for Connor."

He nodded. "That and my promise to Ryan that I'd make sure Connor had a strong male role model in his life."

Skye leaned her elbow on the table and rested her chin on her hand. "I'd say you've honored your promise. We appreciate everything you've done, and Connor adores you."

"I think he's pretty awesome, too." Gage swallowed hard against the emotion clogging his throat at the mention of the little boy, who now took up so much space in his heart. How would he ever be able to say goodbye? What if he'd worked hard to keep his promise to Ryan but lost Connor after all?

The waiter approached to collect the check, and Gage slid his credit card into the leather folder and handed it to him.

"Thank you for dinner, and for coming to Denver to see me." Skye's eyes glistened. "It means a lot."

"You're welcome." This sounded like the beginning of a goodbye. A rush of adrenaline pulsed through him. He didn't want it to end. Sure, they'd see each other in a couple of days when he came to the house to watch Connor, but he sensed it wouldn't be the same. "Can I walk you back to your car? We've got a two-hour drive ahead of us, right?"

"Oh." She averted her gaze and reached for her phone. "I'm actually staying the night at my apartment. I have a breakfast meeting with my boss about a promotion he'd like me to consider."

Her words landed like a gut punch. A promotion. Her boss. His mind raced, and reality closed in fast. "You're planning on moving back here soon?"

She glanced up from her phone. "Right after Easter. My leave is almost over."

Right after Easter. A month from today.

"Wait. What about Connor?" He clenched his fists in his lap. What about *him*? Had today meant nothing?

"I'm not sure McKenna will come home, or if she even wants to. When I move back, I'll have to enroll Connor in day care full-time because he can't stay with my mom or my brothers long-term. I'm assuming Ryan's parents will sue for custody or visitation, but it will be several months until there's a hearing."

The waiter returned with Gage's credit card and receipt. "Thank you, sir. Enjoy your evening."

"Yeah, thanks." Gage dismissed him, still distracted by Skye's news.

"What about the furniture store? Is your brother going to take over when you leave?" It wasn't any of his business, really, but he couldn't fathom her leaving Merritt's Crossing or the budding relationship they'd forged in recent weeks. How could she dismiss him so easily?

She slipped her arms into her coat. "I've told Mom and my brothers that the furniture store isn't viable financially. We are trying to come up with a plan to save the business, but it isn't going to be easy. Mom and Drew think we can still turn things around, especially with so many new families moving here."

He slumped back in his chair. She'd thought of everything. No mention of him, though.

"My Uber's waiting outside." Skye stood and looped her purse strap over her shoulder. "Walk out with me?"

"Yeah, sure." He stood and grabbed his jacket, trying to conceal his hurt.

Outside, a gray sedan idled at the curb.

"That's my ride." Skye turned, went up on tiptoe and pecked him on the cheek.

"Skye—" The intoxicating scent of her perfume enveloped him, and he reached for her, his hand barely skimming her jacket sleeve before she pulled away.

She bit her lip and walked backward toward the car. "Thanks again. For everything. See you Tuesday?"

He could only nod, his stomach plummeting as she climbed into the backseat and slammed the door. The driver's turn signal blinked and he waited to merge into the oncoming traffic. Gage shoved his hands in his pockets and stared after her until the car turned the corner and drove out of sight.

Why was he surprised she'd politely reconstructed her protective shield? His efforts to build a relationship with her—something more meaningful than just their mutual concern for Connor—were no match for her fierce need for independence. After spending a day in her world—the trendy shops and boutiques, fantastic restaurants, a lakefront park two blocks away—why would she choose a quiet life in Merritt's Crossing with him? But he wasn't giving up, especially now that he knew McKenna was battling an addiction. He'd fought his whole life to overcome the pain inflicted by his mom's choices, the people who enabled her and the absence of his father. Gage didn't want Connor to suffer like he had. Even if a relationship with Skye wasn't possible, Gage was more determined than ever to be a part of Connor's life.

Chapter Thirteen

"How was your date with Gage?" Laramie sat cross-legged on Mom's sofa and munched on pretzel sticks.

"It wasn't a date." Skye helped Connor into his pajamas with the fire truck pattern. As usual, he tried his best to resist her efforts.

"Um, there were flowers involved, a walk beside the lake and dinner at your favorite restaurant." Laramie ticked each off on her fingertips. "Was there any kissing involved?"

"Nope, no kisses." She helped Connor sit up. "C'mon, buddy. It's time for a bottle of milk."

Connor pressed a sloppy kiss against his chubby hand and flung it in Laramie's direction.

Skye's breath hitched. He was so precious.

"Well, aren't you the cutest thing ever." Laramie's green eyes gleamed as she blew Connor a kiss in return.

Skye picked up the bottle of milk she'd warmed before she'd changed him and sat down near Laramie in the recliner. With Connor snuggled close, she rocked softly and offered him the bottle.

"It's probably about time to wean him from this, but I just can't." Skye smiled down at him, love and affection spreading through her. These quiet moments with him in her arms, fresh and clean from his bath, had become a part of the day she looked forward to. It was hard to imagine giving that up, especially if she didn't have many bedtimes left with him.

Meeting Mr. and Mrs. Simmons confirmed the truth she'd circled around for several days but refused to admit to anyone—she didn't want Connor to go live with his grandparents, and she didn't want McKenna to come for him. The little boy had won her over and she was terrified of losing him.

"Are you going to share any more details about your not-date with Gage, or am I going to have to fill in the gaps with my imagination?"

Skye forced herself to quit staring at Connor's cherubic face and meet Laramie's curious gaze instead. "It didn't turn out like I'd expected."

Laramie's brow furrowed. "Yeah, you don't seem like someone who had a great time. What happened?"

It was true. She wasn't acting like a woman who'd spent an amazing afternoon and evening with a gorgeous, considerate guy. Tossing and turning in her bed at her apartment last night, she'd mentally rehashed the details, trying to pinpoint when exactly her anxiety spiked. "We had a wonderful time together. The weather was nice, and we had time to process our visit with Connor's grandparents. He told me more about his backstory, and I said some things I—I don't normally share."

"It sounds pretty awesome so far." Laramie reached for her can of soda on the coffee table. "Where did it go wrong?"

"Somewhere between meeting at the coffee shop and dinner, I got really scared." Skye swallowed hard.

"Once I was back in the neighborhood, saw the pace of life and stopped by my apartment, I…I don't know. Something was off."

"You started thinking about what you might be missing, didn't you?"

Skye hesitated. How to explain her feelings without sounding totally self-absorbed? "Gage is a wonderful guy, and I can feel myself falling for him. But at the same time, I don't want to lose my independence. I worked hard for my career. My boss is offering me an incredible promotion. On the other hand, McKenna texted me that she's in rehab, and I don't know if she'll ever be back. I love Connor, too. It's more than feeling obligated to do what is best—I want to find a way to be his mom."

Laramie's eyes widened, and she slowly set her drink back on the coaster. "Did you say any of this to Gage?"

Skye shook her head. "I told him about McKenna and the possibility of a promotion, and that I was leaving Merritt's Crossing right after Easter."

Laramie gasped. "But what about him? Doesn't he factor into your future plans?"

Skye sneaked a quick glance toward the hallway. Last she'd checked, Mom was in the extra bedroom working on a quilting project. Skye leaned closer to Laramie and lowered her voice. "What if I have to hire an attorney to keep Ryan's parents from gaining full custody? Who do you think is going to have to pay those fees? The furniture store is struggling. I can't quit my job now."

Laramie bit her lip. "I didn't realize Connor's grandparents wanted to be actively involved in his life."

"They know McKenna isn't in the best shape to be a full-time mother, and money doesn't seem to be an issue, so I expect we'll be in court soon. I don't mind if they want frequent visitation, but I'm afraid what they want is custody. And if McKenna isn't fit to be a mother, why wouldn't the judge rule in their favor?"

"I'm so sorry." Laramie shook her head. "What a mess."

"That's why I started to backpedal with Gage. By the end of the evening, I couldn't get into my Uber fast enough."

"What if you and Gage become a thing? Isn't that an option? Then you'd have a better chance of getting custody."

"We aren't going to 'become a thing,' not after the way I blew him off."

"I don't know," Laramie said softly. "I've seen the way Gage looks at you."

Skye shook her head. "We can't be a couple just so Connor has two parents. That's crazy."

Wasn't it?

Even if McKenna terminated her parental rights, Gerald and Irene weren't going to give up without a legal battle. What if Gage only wanted her if he could have Connor, too?

"Lots of people marry for convenience," Laramie said. "Remember all those mail-order bride novels my grandmother loves to read? It sounds romantic to me."

She glanced down at Connor, who was chugging the last of his bottle, eyelids growing heavy. He was adorable, and she'd learned to care for him and anticipate his needs, and even adapted to his squealing and affection for grabbing her hair. Her heart swelled. She really did love the little guy.

But could she be his mom? Was she ready for that kind of forever commitment?

"I'd better put him to bed." Skye pushed to her feet and set the bottle on the coffee table. "Are you going to hang out for a minute?"

"No, I have to go. I'm house-sitting for a friend, and their puppy's been in his crate for more than two hours." Laramie stood and put on her jacket. "Skye, I really do think Gage cares for you. Regardless of what happens with Connor, I hope you won't let the allure of Denver or your fears ruin a shot at a potentially wonderful relationship."

"I'm not letting fear ruin anything," Skye protested, her tone harsher than she intended.

Hurt flashed in Laramie's eyes. "Talk to you soon."

After Laramie left, pulling the door closed behind her, Skye blew out a long breath and carried Connor to his bedroom. She didn't want to be afraid—afraid of a man trying to control her again, afraid of Connor not having a stable mom or dad, afraid of hurting Gage any more than she already had. Despite all her efforts to be strong and self-sufficient, she felt just as helpless and overwhelmed as ever.

Was this what he really wanted?

Alone at the Tomlinsons' kitchen table, Gage's hand hovered over the green submit icon on his computer screen. He'd just completed his last module for his online training certification. One click would send his exam to the instructor and he'd move another step closer to his goal.

His professional goal anyway. On a personal note, he was pretty much a wreck.

What if becoming a wind energy technician kept him from being a part of Connor's life? If Connor moved away—especially to Chicago with the Simmonses—

accepting a job in Colorado or Wyoming didn't do him any good. Did keeping his word to Ryan include leading his parents to Connor? Was that genuinely what Ryan wanted? If he did, wouldn't he have made those arrangements or at the very least, told his parents he had a child?

Gage's stomach burned at the thought of Gerald and Irene raising Connor. The little guy's belly laughs and toothy grins, even his feisty side, had worked their way into Gage's heart. Not seeing him take his first steps or hear his first words seemed unimaginable now.

On the other hand, waiting around and letting other people's actions dictate his future wasn't an option, either. McKenna, Ryan's parents and the justice system might all influence where Connor lived next and who he spent time with. Gage had zero control.

Adrenaline surged as he clicked the icon and submitted his exam.

There. At least he could control that.

He returned to a website he'd searched for earlier—the apartment listings for a community closest to the wind farm in Wyoming. It seemed like a nice small town, not too far from Cheyenne. Rent was reasonable, the building looked new and the amenities were better than what he had access to now. He'd even heard rumors that Alta Vista offered a generous signing bonus to new employees.

But it was more than four hours from Denver and even farther from Merritt's Crossing. Half a day's drive—at least—from Skye, which meant they'd rarely see one another if he moved to Wyoming.

Another tab he'd left open on his laptop drew his gaze back to the screen and his stomach clenched. It was a website featuring the Washington Park area in

Denver. For a few glorious minutes, he'd entertained the crazy idea that he and Skye might have a second and a third or even a fourth date. His imagination ran ahead, envisioning another meal at an intimate table in one of her favorite restaurants, her long hair spilling over her shoulders and those gorgeous blue eyes riveted on him, her chin resting on her hand. Later, they'd walk and talk some more, fingers entwined and—

He slammed his laptop closed and scrubbed his hand across his face.

All make-believe. He was an idiot to think he'd legitimately had a shot at a meaningful relationship with Skye. She'd made that clear when she'd rushed to her waiting Uber.

Meeting Skye was an unexpected blessing in his singular quest to find Connor. After spending months focused on his grief and guilt, she was like a burst of sunshine breaking through tumultuous storm clouds. Her obvious distrust had only made him want to prove to her that he was trustworthy. That he wouldn't hurt her.

Instead, she'd wounded him deeply by allowing him to get close, only to push him away. Determined to win her heart, he'd left himself wide-open to her brush-off.

Idiot.

He stood and moved to the sliding glass door and stared out into their backyard, willing the old familiar pain of rejection to go away. Although he'd learned to compartmentalize over the years, Ryan's passing and now his hurt and confusion over Skye dredged up the same emotions he'd tried to stuff deep down.

Rain pelted the crocuses and daffodils poking up near the concrete patio slab and he pressed his palm to the glass.

Why? Why hadn't he seen this coming?

Lord, I trust You. I believe Your ways are better than mine. This still doesn't make any sense, though. Please don't let this innocent child suffer any more than he already has.

The rain fell harder, and while Gage knew his prayers were heard, he didn't feel a sense of peace about Connor or Skye. But standing here feeling sorry for himself wouldn't change anything. Skye and Mrs. Tomlinson were both at the furniture store. They'd finally let him stay with Connor alone. How ironic. Since Connor hadn't woken from his nap yet, Gage needed to make better use of his time. The Wyoming job was only a possibility if he actually applied.

His brain stubbornly refused to fixate on anything other than Skye, though. He pivoted from the window and padded into the kitchen and poured himself another cup of coffee. While her physical beauty had certainly played a role in his initial attraction, her loyalty to her family had both terrified and wooed him.

Since he'd only known the unpredictable and often-frightening roller coaster that was his mother, the Tomlinsons' unwavering commitment to one another seemed foreign at first.

Until he caught himself wondering what it might be like if he was at the center of that devotion.

Unexpected emotion welled up and clogged his throat. He swallowed a sip of the hot liquid, nearly scorching his tongue. Good. If his brain could only process one pain impulse at a time, he'd rather focus on his mouth as opposed to his aching heart.

The fleeting glimpses of Skye's genuine faithfulness to the small number of people she allowed inside her inner circle had made him believe he had somehow earned a place in that circle, too.

And just like every other time he'd put himself out there in a romantic relationship, Skye proved to him that he couldn't have been more wrong.

"Da-da."

Gage froze, coffee mug halfway to his lips, and darted a glance toward the baby monitor on the counter.

"Da-da."

Again. Stronger this time. Connor's voice filtered through the speaker. Gage's pulse sped. That was the closest thing he'd heard to a first word in all the time they'd spent together. He left his mug on the counter and quickly strode to Connor's room.

When he pushed open the door, Connor stood in his crib, chubby hands gripping the rail.

"Da-da!" Connor pointed at Gage and offered that slobbery grin that made Gage almost melt into a puddle. Warmth flooded his chest. Even if it was a coincidence and Connor had no idea what he was saying, it was a bittersweet moment and one he'd always savor, even if he never heard it again.

"Hey, buddy." Gage crossed the bedroom and lifted Connor into his arms. "Let me tell you a story about your daddy."

Chapter Fourteen

Eight days before Easter. Skye tried not to think about her unofficial deadline as she crossed the parking lot, with Connor in her arms wearing sneakers, jeans and a navy blue sweatshirt with a hood he refused to keep on his head.

The blue sky dotted with wispy white clouds arched over the crowd gathering outside of Merritt's Crossing Community Church for the annual Easter festival. While plenty of snow remained, fresh blades of green grass tinged the wheat-colored lawn now sprinkled with hundreds of plastic eggs. Sunshine bathed the whole scene in a golden glow, yet the breeze still carried a bite. Skye was grateful she'd layered her favorite lavender sweater over a white T-shirt and paired tall brown boots with her skinny jeans.

Gage walked beside her, although he said very little. They'd reverted to their businesslike transactions with one another, and once in a while, she caught a glimpse of the hurt lingering in his eyes when he looked at her. It was better this way—pretending their kiss outside Pizza Etc. and special evening together in Denver had never happened.

He surveyed the people milling about. "Do you know where the babies and toddlers are supposed to go?"

"Over there." Skye pointed to a sign designating age groups. "There's a separate egg hunt for kids two and under."

This felt almost like a family outing. Almost. Could she make a life here? If Gage wanted her? She chased the thought away. Even though McKenna hadn't contacted her again and the Simmonses' attorney hadn't served any papers, Skye still clung to her plans not to stay in Merritt's Crossing. Besides, he didn't say that he wanted to be with her. He'd barely said anything at all.

"Let's get in line. I don't want him to miss out." Gage pressed his hand gently against Skye's back and guided her toward the parents clustered with strollers nearby. Warmth radiated through her at his thoughtful gesture. He wasn't steering or controlling or commandeering the situation. She felt safe, cared for with Gage at her side. It had been a long time since she'd experienced that sense of security and comfort with a man. She braced for the old familiar worry to close in, but this time it didn't come. If she was honest, her feelings toward Gage were beginning to outweigh her desire for accepting the promotion. And Laramie's wise words about not letting fear get in the way of a wonderful relationship had stayed with her. Was Denver truly where she needed to be?

She was reaching into the diaper bag for her phone to take pictures when someone grabbed her arm.

"Skye, she's here." Laramie's voice was breathless. "What?"

"McKenna. She's here. I saw her getting out of a car." Skye's stomach plummeted. McKenna was here?

With no text or phone call or warning? She looked at Gage. A muscle in his jaw twitched.

"What do you want to do?" he asked.

"Is she—" Skye shifted Connor to her shoulder, as if turning him away might shield him from whatever came next. "Is she with anyone?"

"I don't think so." Laramie glanced over her shoulder. "But she's coming this way."

Longing for reassurance, or maybe just the comfort of his presence, Skye reached over and wedged one hand in the crook of Gage's elbow. He glanced down at her, his eyes filled with uncertainty.

"We'll figure this out," he said, although his expression revealed he was wrestling with his own doubts.

Skye craned her neck to see around Laramie. Sure enough, McKenna wove her way among the people gathering on the lawn, slowing occasionally to speak to someone. All the while her eyes scanned the crowd. As she moved closer, Skye surveyed her appearance, as if some outward sign of her addiction would confirm or deny her worthiness to be a mother. It was dumb and insensitive, but Skye couldn't help it. She needed to know it was safe for Connor to see McKenna.

In jeans with a ripped knee, cowboy boots and a flowery tunic layered under a denim jacket, she looked like a typical twentysomething female at a small-town festival. When she looked up and met Skye's gaze, her steps faltered.

"Hey." McKenna's brown eyes flitted from Skye to Gage and then landed on Connor. Surprise flashed across her features, and then her mouth formed a wobbly smile. "I'm back."

"I see that." Skye choked out the words. "What are you doing here?"

"Skye." Laramie's voice was tinged with warning.

McKenna's gaze narrowed. "I came for my son."

Connor whined and twisted in Skye's arms, as if to see what the delay was all about. He regarded McKenna with a wide-eyed stare.

"Hey, cutie pie." McKenna stretched out her arms. "Come see Mama."

"Wait. Think of the baby. He hasn't seen you in months." Skye angled her body away from McKenna, desperate to reason with her. "Please, don't do this."

"He's mine. I've come all this way like you asked me to, so why won't you let me have my son?"

"Because we're not confident you can handle him," Gage said, his voice low.

McKenna stared at him. "I remember you—you're Ryan's friend." She smirked. "How nice of you to step up and play pretend baby daddy."

Skye sucked in a breath. Her legs trembled, and spots peppered her vision. Even though she'd hoped for weeks that McKenna would come back, so much had changed. She loved Connor like her own, and now she didn't want McKenna to take him.

"McKenna, please." Laramie stepped between them and placed a hand on McKenna's arm. "Why don't we take Connor to the egg hunt—all of us together—and then we can meet afterward and try to work this out?"

"Let go of me." McKenna pulled from her grasp. "I don't need your help, either. Just give me my kid."

"We only want what's best for you and Connor," Laramie said softly.

"You have no right to keep him from me."

"You're right, we don't." Hot tears pricked her eyes as Skye handed Connor to McKenna.

His face crumpled, and he began to cry.

"Do you want his car seat?" Skye swallowed hard against the lump clogging her throat and glanced down at the diaper bag. "Do you have diapers and wipes?"

"Where are you staying?" Laramie asked.

"I've got a place. You don't have to worry." She smiled at Connor and shushed him, awkwardly bouncing him up and down.

He twisted in her embrace and stretched his arms toward Skye.

Her heart cleaved in two. This couldn't be happening.

"You don't really expect us to just let you drive off with a baby, do you?" Gage's voice held a hard edge.

Skye bit her lip, desperate to hold herself together for Connor's sake. She glanced at Gage. He'd straightened to his full, very imposing height and wore a granitelike expression, while his icy gaze bored into McKenna.

McKenna shifted the very distraught Connor to her other shoulder and tipped her chin defiantly. "He's mine. You can't stop me."

"What happens when he won't stop crying? When you blow all your cash on booze and don't have any left for food? Do you even know what he eats?" Gage raised his voice, hands clenched at his sides, drawing curious glances from the onlookers forming a half circle around them in the parking lot.

"Gage." Skye touched his arm with her hand. "Settle down."

"You can't tell me what to do with my own kid." McKenna's eyes glittered. "Thanks for everything, Skye. Don't worry, I've got this."

"How about an attorney? Do you have one of those retained, too?" Gage growled.

"Stop," Skye said.

McKenna pushed through the crowd and strode toward a small economical car parked at the edge of the lot. Connor's wailing rose above the buzz of conversation.

Skye whirled and faced Gage, tears streaming from her eyes. "You shouldn't have confronted her."

"Really?" Gage stared at her in disbelief. "You're blaming me for this?"

"You're the one who yelled at her."

"Because you just stood there and let her take Connor. What else was I supposed to do? Stand back and do nothing while you tried to reason with her?"

"It's better than yelling."

"No. It's not." Anger flashed in his eyes. "You can't reason with an addict."

"She's recovered." Skye swiped at her cheeks with the cuff of her sleeve.

"How do you know?" Gage's chest heaved, his fists still clenched at his sides. "Did you even ask her if she'd completed her rehab? What if she stole that car?"

Skye wanted to throw up. She just shrugged helplessly. "Trying to talk some sense into her is better than yelling."

"Let me ask you this —all those years you and your family spent trying to talk some sense into her." He quoted the air with his fingers. "Did it work? Maybe if you-all weren't so loyal to one another, things might be different. But now she's leaving, with a baby who has no idea who she is, and we don't have a clue where she's headed."

Reeling from his harsh words, Skye stared at him, her body shaking. "Wh-what did you say?"

Gage huffed out a breath and shook his head. "I can't stand here and watch you fall apart." He turned and jogged toward his truck. "I'm going to follow her," he called over his shoulder.

Skye leaned into Laramie's embrace, sobbing. Why did he flip out and blame this on her?

Skye was out of her mind.

Gage clenched his jaw until it hurt. Her ability to enable McKenna had sunk to a new low today.

How could she tell him he shouldn't have *yelled*? Somebody needed to get through to McKenna, and it sure wasn't going to be Skye—not when she handed the baby over like a sack of groceries. Gage gripped his steering wheel tighter and forced himself to concentrate as he trailed McKenna's small white car to a new neighborhood on the edge of town—the one where a lot of the new Alta Vista Energy employees had bought homes.

Where was she getting the money to cover a mortgage or a month's rent? Had she hooked up with some new guy already? The thought of yet another stranger spending time with Connor spiked fear in his gut.

It was all he could do not to jump out of his truck and confront her again.

Instead, he kept a safe distance and left the engine running while he tracked her every move through his windshield. She parked and got out, then carefully lifted Connor into her arms and carried him, along with the diaper bag Skye gave her, toward the front of the house. His view was obstructed by shrubs and the corner of the two-car garage, so he couldn't see who answered the door or if she had a key of her own.

A few minutes later, he slowly drove by the house and snapped a quick picture of her license plate and made a note of the street address. He'd already called Drew, who'd confirmed that while he wasn't thrilled with his cousin's actions, no laws were violated. Mc-Kenna had every right to take her child, whether they thought she was capable of being a mother or not. Unless she endangered her child or committed a crime, there was nothing they could do.

Nothing they could do.

He scraped his hand across his face and slowly accelerated, while a hollow ache settled in his chest. Although he couldn't hang around and spy on McKenna, it physically hurt to drive away knowing Connor was inside with her. Was he still crying? Did he have any idea who she was? Who else was in the house with them?

The same unanswered questions spun through his mind—even if she was his mother, what if she didn't know how to take care of a one-year-old? She hadn't smelled like alcohol when they saw her at the festival, and she'd appeared sober and lucid. Still—he couldn't believe this was happening. So what if she was his mother? They shouldn't have allowed Connor to go with her.

Back at his own apartment, he reached for his phone to call Skye and tell her what he'd observed, and then he hesitated. She was angry. Distraught. The hurt and disbelief in her eyes when he'd told her what he really thought was an image he wouldn't soon forget. He put his phone away and started pacing. He was angry, too. If it weren't for the way her family had handled this whole situation, Connor might still be—

A knock sounded at his door. His boots clomped across the floor as he crossed his apartment in quick strides. A peek out the peephole revealed Drew waiting on the other side. In jeans, a hooded sweatshirt and a ball cap, he didn't look like he was on official business from the sheriff's department. So why was he here?

"Hey," Gage greeted him, his heart kicking against his rib cage. He knew it. McKenna had blown it already, just like he feared. "What happened?"

Drew's brows arched. "Take it easy. I'm just stopping by to check on you."

Oh. Gage crossed his arms over his chest. "So no updates, then."

"Not that I know of. Mind if I come in?"

Gage stepped back without saying anything. Drew walked inside and glanced around. Gage closed the door behind him. An awkward silence filled the air as they stood in the entryway, staring each other down. It wasn't like Gage planned to offer him a soda or anything. This was hardly the time to kick back and watch a ball game together.

Drew cleared his throat. "I ran the plates on McKenna's car. She didn't steal it. My aunt Willa is the owner."

Of course she is. Gage swallowed back the snarky reply. That wasn't fair. He didn't know McKenna or her mother, but he couldn't help chalking it up to one more way the family had enabled McKenna to get whatever she wanted.

"How about the place where she's staying—whose house is that?" Gage asked.

"No clue." Drew removed his ball cap and swiped his palm across his face. "I know this has been a tough day—for everybody—and I wanted to make sure you were all right."

What? How could he possibly be all right? Gage narrowed his gaze. "It's hard to imagine how anyone could hand over an innocent child—a baby—to the same woman who abandoned him."

Drew sighed and tugged his cap back into place, ignoring Gage's barb at his family. "Like I said, she didn't break any laws. We can't keep her from her own kid."

"What if she leaves again? Or—or worse, leaves Connor with a total stranger?" Blood whooshed in Gage's ears. How did Drew stay so calm—so matter-of-fact—about all this? They didn't know who McKenna was with or how she was planning to provide for herself and a helpless child.

"We are going to hope and pray that this time she's got her act together and she'll do what's best for herself and for Connor."

Gage scoffed. "I gotta be honest, I'm not real optimistic."

Drew pursed his lips. "Look, you're fired up about this, and your feelings are justified, but I—"

"If you know I'm right, then why not do something about it?" Gage's voice rose an octave, but he didn't care.

"I told you, there's nothing I can do."

"What about Skye? She hasn't asked you to intervene, either?"

Empathy filled Drew's eyes. He paused and then shook his head. "She didn't ask me to come here, if that's what you're asking."

Ouch. While he suspected that was the case, it didn't hurt any less to hear Drew confirm it. Probably shouldn't have asked if he didn't want to hear the answer. Gage brushed past him and opened the door. If Drew wasn't here to help, then there wasn't much left to say. "Let me know if you hear anything."

"Gage—"

"Thanks for stopping by."

Drew jammed his hands in the front pocket of his hoodie and left without another word. Gage stood there, staring at the closed door, a sickening sensation in his gut. Connor was going to spend the night in an unfamiliar place with a woman who was his mother, but basically a stranger, and there wasn't one thing Gage could do about it.

"I'm sorry, little buddy," he whispered, his voice breaking. "This wasn't supposed to happen. I'm going to fix it, I promise."

Tears stung the backs of his eyes and he wedged the heels of his palms against them to staunch the flow. He feared his words, like so many times before, were empty promises he couldn't deliver. He'd failed Connor just like he'd failed Ryan.

The house was way too quiet.

Skye sat on the sofa next to Mom and dabbed at her eyes with a tissue. How could the absence of one little boy make her cry so much?

"I'm proud of you, sweetie. You did the best you could." Mom patted her leg. "This is all in the Lord's hands now."

Was it? She hadn't relied on the Lord much lately. Sure, she believed all those things she'd learned in Sunday school growing up and felt gratitude for her many blessings, but that was the extent of her relationship with Him. If He loved them, why had Connor— all of them, really—lost so much?

"I can't believe Gage." Skye huffed out a breath. "First of all, he yelled at me, which was completely out of character, and then, as if that wasn't enough, he blamed you and me and—and our whole family for McKenna's behavior."

The ticking of the mantel clock filled the silence.

"Mmm."

Her mother's empathetic murmur got under Skye's skin. "Don't tell me you agree with him."

"I do."

"What?" Skye stared at her. "How?"

"The feud between Uncle Kenny and your father impacted all of us, including McKenna," Mom said. "Your aunt Willa did the best she could, but Kenny's rage was all consuming. He truly believed your dad had deprived him of a fortune."

Skye scoffed. "I don't know about a fortune, but Dad sure made some lousy choices about money."

"True. I wish I'd known sooner." Mom smoothed her hand over Skye's hair. "I'm not much different than your aunt Willa after all. Maybe I didn't want to see the truth about your dad, either. By the time she realized McKenna's wild ways, it was too late."

Skye twisted her crumpled tissue between her fingers. "It's not our fault she ran off and got pregnant, though."

"No, it isn't. She bears some responsibility in bringing Connor into this world." Mom sighed. "Now that I've lost your dad and we've learned he harbored secrets of his own, I have more empathy and grace for people and their struggles."

Skye winced. Too bad she couldn't embrace Mom's perspective. It just hurt too much.

"What happened to you?" Mom reached for Skye's hand. "Somebody must've done or said something terrible. You seem…closed off. Do you want to talk about it?"

Skye pressed her lips together and a fresh wave of shame washed over her.

"You can tell me anything. You know that, right?"

Skye drew a ragged breath. "A guy I dated for a while, he—he was very cruel."

Mom stiffened. "Oh, Skye."

"With his words, not with his fists." She forced herself to look at her mom. "But I don't ever want to feel that intimidated or belittled again."

"Sweetheart, I am so sorry." Tears glistened in Mom's eyes. "Why didn't you tell me?"

She ducked her head. "At first, I was embarrassed because I should've known better than to date someone who didn't treat me well. Then ashamed and afraid of what people might say or think."

"Your brothers and I, we wouldn't shame you. We love you and we are so proud of you. There's nothing you could tell us that changes how we feel."

"I—I know." Skye rested her head against her mother's and more tears tracked down her cheeks.

"Have you spoken to anyone else about this—your pastor or a counselor?"

"I saw a therapist in Denver." Skye sniffed. "That helped a lot. She told me I didn't need to see her while I was staying here."

Silence filled the air. Skye's pulse sped. Did Mom disapprove of her decision to get professional help? Tentatively, her gaze swung toward her mother.

Tenderness filled her eyes. "Have you felt comfortable dating anyone else?"

"Mom." Skye didn't bother to keep the irritation from her voice. She looked away. What happened to empathy and compassion for people and their struggles? She knew exactly where this discussion was going.

"Gage is a wonderful man, and he's a natural with Connor."

"I can't be with someone who loses their temper in a crisis."

Mom shifted to face Skye. "Perhaps his anger wasn't directed at you but more at the circumstances. He—"

Skye shot her a warning look. "He yelled at me. In front of everyone. And he said it was our fault for being too loyal."

Mom's lips formed an O. "We all say things we don't mean sometimes in the heat of the moment."

Skye bit back a snide remark. It wasn't that simple.

"I suppose this means you'll be going back to Denver after Easter," Mom said quietly.

Skye's stomach knotted tight. "I think that would be best. My boss isn't obligated to hold my job open, and I don't see how I can turn things around at the furniture store."

"No one expects you to rescue the store all by yourself."

Skye studied her. "Are you sure?"

"Positive." Mom's smile was sad. "The store had a good, long run. Times are changing here. My hope is that business will improve, or somehow we'll transform that building into a space that benefits the community."

"Even if the store does close, part of me feels like I should stick around because I'm not sure McKenna will be able to handle full-time motherhood." Skye tipped her head back and stared at the ceiling. "But I can't keep her from her son."

"You need to follow your heart," Mom said. "My knee is much better, and I'll be able to drive again starting Monday. I want you to be free to make the decision that's best for you."

A fresh wave of tears threatened to fall, and Skye's

vision blurred as she offered Mom a smile. "Then I'll leave for Denver after our Easter brunch."

With Mom's blessing, she'd return to work, get settled in her Denver apartment and reconnect with her friends. After the way Gage had treated her at the festival, she didn't want to speak to him or even see him again. Now that Connor and McKenna had reunited, there was no reason to extend her stay in Merritt's Crossing.

Chapter Fifteen

❧

Gage tugged at his starched collar and gravel crunched under his black wing tips as he strode across the parking lot at Alta Vista Energy Group on Thursday afternoon. Man, he couldn't wait to get to his truck and loosen his tie. The sun slanted through the trees, which displayed tiny green buds, hinting that spring might've finally arrived. Birds chirped, and he didn't need a winter jacket for the first time in months.

Newly certified as a wind energy technician, his first job interview had gone well. The hiring manager said he'd get back to him soon. While he had a lot to be thankful for, regret and sadness over the absence of Connor and Skye weighed him down.

"There he is." Max's voice derailed the beginning of Gage's pity party.

Max climbed out of his truck nearby and waved. "Congratulations, by the way. I hear you had an interview."

"Thanks." Gage darted a glance to the back of the truck, where Dane was unloading equipment. They hadn't seen much of each other since their contentious air hockey duel. It was probably for the best. If they ended up being coworkers or even partners, he'd have to have a conversation about that night. Dane tipped his chin with the obligatory nod, then disappeared into the garage.

"Has anyone else offered you a job?" Max asked.

"Not yet. This is my first interview," Gage said. "I applied for an opening in Wyoming, too."

"Well that's a no-brainer." Max chuckled. "Merritt's Crossing is much better than the middle of nowhere in Wyoming."

Gage didn't answer.

"Unless you like the middle of nowhere." Max scrambled to recover. "Some folks do, I suppose."

Thoughts of Skye and Connor flitted through his head. "I've got some time to think about it—weigh the pros and cons."

Max nodded. "Anyone would be fortunate to have you on their team."

"Thanks, Max." Gage smiled. "I appreciate that."

Max glanced at his watch. "The grandkids are driving down from Boulder today, so I'd better get home. Any Easter plans?"

"Not really."

None, actually. Gage looked away. Spending the holiday alone wasn't his idea of fun, but he didn't need Max feeling sorry for him, too.

"Why don't you come over to our place? Lots of kids, tons of food—my wife's been cooking all week. We'd love to have you."

Gage hesitated. "I don't want to impose."

"No imposition. Come to think of it, why don't you come by at nine and go to church with us? We belong to a little country church near Limon. Great people."

"All right. I'll be there."

"Good. I'll let my wife know." Max clapped him on the shoulder, his eyes twinkling. "See you then."

"Thanks, Max. I really appreciate it."

"Not a problem."

They said goodbye and Gage strode toward his truck parked on the other side of the lot. Easter was only three days away. Hard to believe less than a week had passed since McKenna had taken Connor. His heart felt hollow. He missed the little guy. Skye, too. He hadn't seen or heard from any of the Tomlinsons since Drew's visit to his apartment. While he'd driven by the house where McKenna was supposedly staying more than once, he'd intentionally avoided Skye.

It hurt too much.

Gage shed his suit coat and loosened his tie before getting behind the wheel of his truck. While he turned the key in the ignition, his gaze swung to Ryan's photo on the dash.

"Sorry, man," Gage whispered. "I messed this all up."

He'd said those words a lot lately. The end result was still the same: Ryan was gone and Connor didn't have a dad. Gritting his teeth, Gage drove away, his promise to Ryan playing on endless repeat in his head. How could he keep his word if McKenna didn't let him be involved in Connor's life?

As he passed the grocery store, his foot pressed harder on the accelerator, his mind rehashing last night's conversation when he'd bumped into Laramie in the dairy aisle. She'd mentioned that Skye planned to go back to work next week in Denver. The news struck like a fist to his gut. He hadn't been able to stop thinking about her, or the harsh words he'd spewed at the festival.

Max was wrong.

He deserved the middle of nowhere. Alone. Because he totally blew it with Skye. He shouldn't have accused her of being too loyal. If it weren't for Skye's willingness to help her cousin, McKenna might've left Connor with a stranger. Skye's love and faithfulness to her family despite their grief and broken relationships is what kept Connor safe and well cared for.

He'd failed on so many levels.

And now the realization of how much both Connor and Skye meant to him was unbearable. He loved her. Connor, too. Even if he couldn't be a part of Connor's life anymore, he wanted Skye.

Not that she'd ever speak to him again after the horrible things he'd said.

But leaving town without telling her how he felt or at the very least saying goodbye made him feel like a coward.

And he didn't need any more reasons to feel like a coward. He'd already spent weeks—no, make that months—fixating on his guilt and regret over not being able to say goodbye to Ryan or rescue him during the submarine fire. While those feelings had lessened slightly, it was still something he'd carry with him for the rest of his life.

He released a heavy sigh as he slowed to make a turn. What good did it do to stay in Merritt's Crossing now? McKenna seemed determined to care for Connor on her own anyway. The thought of Connor growing up without a positive male influence in his life planted an icy ball of dread in Gage's stomach. Ryan's parents hadn't filed for permanent custody—at least not that he knew of.

If he had a job offer in Merritt's Crossing and stayed, but McKenna took Connor and moved away again, then he was stuck working in this place surrounded by painful reminders of all he'd lost—Skye, Connor and a chance to have a family of his own.

Maybe Wyoming was the better option. His only option now.

Standing under the gazebo in the community park, Skye bowed her head as the pastor prayed the benediction and the Easter sunrise service ended. A breeze blew off the pond, and she shoved her hands deeper in the pockets of her peacoat. If only she could shove aside the lonely ache taking up residence in her heart.

This was her last morning in Merritt's Crossing. The car was packed. After church and brunch with her family, she'd be on her way back to Denver.

Leaving was the right decision, wasn't it?

She turned her face upward to admire the pinks and oranges streaking overhead and savored the hum of quiet conversation buzzing around her as folks greeted each other. Uncle Milt's familiar chuckle wafted through the small crowd and Skye felt a smile tug at her lips. For all the struggles and challenges of small-town life, this would always be home.

"Happy Easter." Laramie walked up beside her, wearing a denim jacket over a yellow dress and a patterned scarf layered around her neck. "Is your family here?"

Skye shook her head. "I came alone. Mom was worried about standing too long, so she's going to the ten fifteen service." She gave her best friend a long look. "Jack didn't come, either, in case you're wondering."

Laramie looked away, two splotches of color darkening her cheeks. "I wasn't wondering."

"Not even a little bit?"

She sighed, then lifted her chin, a hint of mischief glinting in her eyes. "Okay, maybe a little. I do have a thing for that particular handsome, brooding brother of yours."

Skye flung her arm around Laramie's shoulders. "Don't give up. One of these days, he'll come to his senses and see how amazing you are."

"Doubtful but thank you. Too much history there," Laramie said. "Speaking of coming to our senses, have you spoken to Gage lately?"

"No." Her pulse ratcheted at the mention of his name. She'd thought about calling him. The days since the Easter festival crawled by, and every time a car drove past the house, she'd hoped it was Gage. Maybe he was fine with the way things ended. Maybe he'd made peace with the fact that McKenna and Connor were reunited.

Maybe he didn't want her in his life.

That last part was the hardest for her to accept.

"C'mon, let's talk." Laramie's gaze darted around the crowd. "Privately."

Arms linked, they walked slowly across the lawn toward their respective cars. The pastor's message about God being a good Father, one who loved unconditionally and didn't hold her shortcomings against her, still resonated in Skye's mind. Only this time, she let the familiar words blossom and flourish, instead of strangling the life out of them and pretending they didn't apply to her. The realization that she'd allowed so much guilt and resentment to build up, keeping her from fully living—and loving—nearly stole her breath.

"Good message this morning," Laramie said, picking her way through the grass in her peep-toe wedges.

"Uh-huh."

Laramie stopped walking and faced Skye. "I'll spare

you the lecture, but I just want to say one more thing before you pack up and go."

"Don't use what happened with Connor as an excuse to push Gage away?"

Laramie's eyes lit up. "Exactly."

The breeze blew a strand of hair across Skye's cheek and she carefully extracted it from her lipstick and tucked it behind her ear. "I messed up, Lare. I've let my fear hold me back, and now I'm afraid I missed out on a wonderful relationship."

Laramie's expression morphed into one of empathy. "I'm sorry that some of the men in your life have let you down. Everybody is going to mess up and disappoint us. That's part of being human. Gage doesn't seem like he has anything but your best interests in mind."

"I know that now. Now that it's too late." She swallowed back the lump burning in her throat and dipped her chin. "I—I was afraid of losing my independence, and I didn't want to be a victim, too weak to speak my mind or defend myself."

"He might've been angry about McKenna taking Connor and said some things that were hard to hear, but he wasn't demeaning."

"And he was right about our family. We have enabled McKenna in so many ways for such a long time." She cringed, thinking about how their efforts to help had often caused more hurt and dysfunction instead.

"On the upside, what if your independence and fierce love for your family is one of the things he really admires?"

"I'm not sure there's anything he loves about me right now. I was an idiot."

"But you don't have to stay an idiot."

Skye shot her a look. "Aren't you clever."

Laramie grinned. "That's why I'm your best friend." She gently steered Skye toward her car. "Why don't you go tell Gage everything you just told me?"

Skye's breath caught. "Now?"

"Yes, now." Laramie's tone was firm. Resolute. "Rumor has it he has a job interview in Wyoming this week."

Adrenaline surged as she thought about showing up at Gage's apartment, only to have the door slammed firmly in her face.

"I know what you're thinking," Laramie said, hands planted firmly at her waist and the skirt of her dress swirling around her legs. "But isn't the risk of rejection worth the effort?"

Skye hesitated, then nodded slowly.

"That's my girl." Laramie swept her into an enthusiastic hug. "I'm praying for you."

"Thank you. For everything." Skye pulled away, more tears threatening to fall. "What am I going to do in Denver without you?"

Laramie shook her head and held up her palm. "We aren't going there right now. You're on a new mission, remember?"

"Right."

Her heart in her throat, Skye climbed into her car and drove to Gage's apartment. As she strode across the parking lot, she scanned the space for a glimpse of his truck. Nothing. She hadn't called or texted first because she didn't want him to have the opportunity to avoid her. Buoyed by Laramie's pep talk, she hadn't stopped to consider that he might not be home at eight thirty on Easter morning. Had he been at the sunrise service and she'd missed him? That couldn't be. Laramie and her eagle eyes would've noticed.

She knocked on his door and waited. *Please, please, please be here.* Now that she realized how wrong she'd been, she didn't want to wait another minute to apologize and tell him she cared deeply. That somewhere between the babysitting and their evening in Denver, she'd fallen in love with him.

When she knocked again, only silence greeted her.

With a heavy heart, she dug through her purse for a pen and something to write on. A text hardly seemed adequate at this point. All she found was a pen and a receipt from the coffee shop in Denver—the one they'd visited before their walk around the lake. She smiled at the bittersweet memory, scrawled a note asking Gage to call her, then tucked it into the door frame.

She sighed and returned to her car. Maybe this was a lesson learned—her fear had kept her from living openhandedly and receiving the blessing she'd been too guarded and resistant to accept—the love of a strong, devoted, wonderful man. And now it was too late.

Gage set a container full of leftovers from Max's wife on the passenger seat of his truck, then slid behind the wheel and slammed the door. Spending Easter with Max's family was a lot of fun, but he hated that he hadn't spoken to Skye. Now it was too late. She was probably in Denver by now, getting ready for her first day back at work.

And he was alone.

Even the prospect of a road trip to Wyoming and a job interview first thing Monday morning didn't brighten his mood. He huffed out a long breath and angled his truck out of Max's long driveway. Their farmhouse—situated in the middle of several acres about forty-five minutes from town—was stunning, and Gage had enjoyed spending the day with Max and his family.

But it wasn't the same as being with Skye and Connor.

Why hadn't he made the effort to track her down and speak with her? To admit he'd said all the wrong things at the Easter festival, and that he wanted to be a part of her life—with or without Connor? While he'd convinced himself that letting her go was best for both of them, the loneliness and regret were eating him up inside.

The late-afternoon sunshine bathed the cab of his truck in a soft glow, and he reached for his sunglasses. As he merged onto the highway, his thoughts alternated between Skye and Connor. Occasionally, an image of the three of them together again materialized, but he didn't allow himself to dwell there for long. What was the use? She was gone, and he'd been too stubborn to ask her to stay.

Lord, I need help. I don't want to live like this— trapped in my own insecurity.

Up ahead, a vehicle on the side of the road caught his attention, and he merged to the right and slowed down. The small white car sat on the shoulder, its front end angled toward the wire fence dividing the pasture from the highway. As he eased in behind it and surveyed the scene, his heart lurched.

McKenna's car. He'd memorized the license plate number.

"Please, please let them be okay." Gage flung up the prayer, then jumped out of his truck and jogged toward the driver's side. Through the closed windows he could hear Connor crying.

"McKenna!" Gage rapped his knuckles on her window. "Open up."

She glanced up, eyes wide and tears evident on her splotchy cheeks.

Connor caught sight of him and screamed louder.

Adrenaline pulsed through Gage's veins as he grabbed the door handle and tried to open it.

Locked.

McKenna looked down and a second later he heard the automatic locks release. The door sprang open.

"Are you all right?" he asked, scanning her face again for any sign of injury.

"I—I don't— I don't think so." She shook her head and looked around.

Was she in shock?

"What happened?"

Her fingers trembled as she reached up and rubbed her forehead, a gesture that vaguely reminded him of Skye. "I must've fallen asleep for a second."

"I need to get Connor out of his car seat and make sure he's okay." Gage kept his voice calm but firm. Did she really fall asleep? Should he call 911?

She glanced up at him again, her teeth chattering. "Th-th-that would be good."

He hesitated. Were her pupils dilated? He couldn't tell for sure. There wasn't time to interrogate her anyway, not with Connor still screaming from the backseat. He had to make sure the baby was all right.

Gage lunged for the back door and yanked it open, his heart in his throat. Connor's face was red, and tears clung to his lashes. He stretched his arms toward Gage.

"Aw, buddy. It's okay." Gage worked quickly to unfasten the car seat harness. He recognized the fear in Connor's cry and the realization that he'd learned to differentiate made a lump form in Gage's throat. Pulling the little guy into his arms, Gage pressed a kiss to Connor's cheek and then nestled him close to his chest.

Breathing in the scent of baby shampoo, Gage swayed gently, blinking back tears of his own.

"Is he okay?" McKenna asked, swiping at her nose with the back of her hand.

Connor's cries quieted, and he drew several hiccupy breaths, while his fist clung to the lapel of Gage's fleece pullover.

Gage cleared his throat. "I think so." He carefully examined Connor's face and hands. No scrapes, cuts or bruises. He shifted his gaze to check inside the car. When he saw the brown paper bag on the floor, his stomach plummeted.

"McKenna." He could barely choke out her name. Worry shifted to alarm. "What's in the bag?"

She didn't answer.

"McKenna, have you been drinking and driving?"

She shook her head quickly. "I haven't. I promise. You can look, the bottles haven't been opened."

"You shouldn't have alcohol in your car." Gage fought to keep his tone even. He didn't want to lose his temper this time, but he couldn't believe she'd started drinking again. Not when she was solely responsible for Connor.

"I wasn't drinking. Not yet anyway." She pressed her lips together. "On Saturday I—I tried to get my old job back waitressing at the diner in Limon, but they said I had to prove I had reliable child care first."

Connor started to fuss again, and Gage shifted him in his arms and kept swaying gently, hoping to soothe him.

McKenna glanced up at him, squinting in the sunlight. "He isn't very easy for me to take care of, and he isn't sleeping well at night. I—I don't know who to ask to babysit him that I can trust, either."

"That still doesn't explain why you have alcohol in your car."

"I'm getting to that part. After I left the diner, I was upset that they'd told me no. Connor fell asleep in his car seat, so I went into the liquor store and…stocked up." She ducked her head. "But I didn't open them. You have to believe me."

The hum of another vehicle approaching kept Gage from answering. He circled around the front of McKenna's car to find a safer place to stand. The truck slowed, but Gage gave the driver a thumbs-up, and the truck kept moving.

McKenna got out of the car and faced him. She wrapped her arms around her torso. When her gaze met his, he saw only defeat and sorrow etched in her features.

"Will you please drive us to my aunt's house? I think I need her and Skye to take Connor for me."

"Skye's gone."

Surprise popped in McKenna's eyes. "Denver?"

He gritted his teeth and nodded slowly.

McKenna shivered and stared off in the distance. "Can you take me to my aunt's house anyway? I need to find someone to take Connor. Permanently."

Gage's breath caught. "Are you sure?"

She glanced at him again, tears clinging to her eyelashes. "I can't be his mother. At least not the mother he needs and deserves."

"If you'll hold Connor, I'll transfer his car seat to my truck."

"All right."

While Gage got Connor and McKenna situated in his truck and made arrangements to have her car towed, his mind raced ahead to possible scenarios. Skye had said she didn't want to be a mother. Was that still true? Would she change her mind if she knew McKenna was ready to relinquish her rights? Ryan's parents and their attorney would certainly be thrilled to hear the news.

His gut tightened at the thought of Connor moving to Illinois permanently. While he'd promised Ryan he'd look out for Connor, deep down, he didn't believe Gerald and Irene were the best long-term caregivers. As he drove back to Merritt's Crossing, McKenna and Connor both fell asleep, and he relished the peace and quiet, seizing the opportunity to pour out his heart's desire to the Lord. He wanted to be more than a male role model or a family friend. He longed to be Connor's father, and he'd give anything to make that a reality.

Chapter Sixteen

Exhausted, Skye carried the last box of her belongings from the elevator to the door of her apartment in Denver. What a marathon, trying to unpack the car by herself. She fumbled in her handbag for her keys. Her back ached from heaving her overstuffed suitcases in and out of the trunk, and her head felt like it was caught in a vise grip. Even though she didn't start back at work until tomorrow, her stomach twisted as she thought about the impossible-to-meet sales goals, the benefits of a new anti-inflammatory medication she was supposed to start promoting to physicians right away, plus her new territory, which was much larger than her manager had initially indicated.

Suddenly, returning to work didn't seem as exciting as she'd hoped. Right now, she'd give anything for another afternoon at the furniture store and a simple spreadsheet of last year's earnings and expenses. Or another day with Gage and an opportunity to tell him how she truly felt about him. Why had she given up so easily?

Her phone buzzed again, and she groaned. That was probably her manager or her sales team asking her to

meet for dinner tomorrow night. *No, thank you.* She'd
let the call go to voice mail. Just like the six other calls
that came in while she was driving back from Merritt's
Crossing today. Her phone had fallen from the center
console and slid under the passenger seat about forty
minutes into her trip and she'd ignored it the rest of the
way to Denver. All she wanted was to get settled and
take a luxurious bubble bath.

Four more familiar chimes came in quick succession,
indicating a flurry of text messages. Probably not Bethany, her former babysitter. A pang of regret thrummed
at the unexpected reminder of Connor and her time
in Merritt's Crossing. Although she tried not to think
about him, the sweet little fella had stolen a piece of
her heart and was never far from her thoughts. Was he
taking his first steps yet? Did McKenna have a good
job? Was he safe?

She dug her phone from her bag and glanced at the
screen. Ten missed calls and multiple text messages
waited. What in the world?

The first text from Mom made her pulse race.

Connor is here. McKenna wants us to take him. Permanently. Is there any way you could come home??

The next messages from Laramie, Jack and Drew
were all variations on the same piece of shocking news.
The last message from Gage made tears well.

Skye, I found McKenna and Connor on the side of the
highway. If you don't want to text me, I understand,
but please contact your mom ASAP. It's important.
Connor needs you.

"The side of the *highway*?" She quickly scrolled through the messages for more details. What had happened to McKenna? Was she hurt? Was Connor hurt? There were far more questions than answers.

Her hands shook as she attempted to text them all at once. Leaving Denver now.

She quickly shoved the box inside her apartment, grabbed one of the suitcases she'd recently unloaded, locked the door and rushed back to her car. While she navigated the Sunday-evening and holiday traffic, one important question surfaced above all the others. What about Gage? Did he need her? Or was he merely the messenger, dutifully informing her of what he'd observed as a first responder?

As the city lights faded behind her in the rearview mirror and darkness closed in, sheer adrenaline kept her barreling down the interstate toward Merritt's Crossing. It was after nine when she pulled into her mom's driveway, and her headlights bounced across a familiar pickup truck. Gage.

Her pulse skittered as Mom's front door opened and his broad, muscular frame was silhouetted by the light spilling out from the living room. The visual image of him waiting for her—welcoming her home—propelled her out of the car. She left the engine running and raced up the driveway, then flung herself into his open arms.

"I'm so sorry." Her voice broke and she clung to him, her arms roped around his neck and her cheek pressed against his chest.

Gage's strong arms encircled her waist and he held her close, enveloping her, like a shelter in the middle of a brutal storm. Even if McKenna hadn't changed her mind about Connor, Skye would've come back. In her heart, she knew Denver and her career didn't offer happiness and contentment. Gage did. She belonged with him.

This—this felt like home. *He* was her home.

She closed her eyes, the realization prompting a wave of fresh tears, and she earnestly hoped that he felt the same way.

Slowly, she pulled back and searched his face. "Say something. Please."

A half smile formed, and he tenderly wiped away her tears with the pad of his thumb, sending a warm, tingly sensation straight through her.

"I'm glad you're here," he said, his voice husky. "I've missed you so much."

"Will you please forgive me?" She kept her gaze riveted on his. "I was such an idiot, letting my fear stand between us."

"*Idiot* is not a word I would ever use to describe you." The golden glow of the lamplight emphasized the broad planes of his face and he cupped her cheek with his palm. "You are beautiful and intelligent, and your fierce loyalty to the people you love is a force to be reckoned with."

"It's also the thing that gets me in the most trouble, especially when it blinds me to what's right in front of me." She swallowed hard. "I'm so sorry for the things I said at the festival. You were right. We've enabled McKenna for a long time and it wreaked havoc in our lives. And even if she hadn't changed her mind, I'm here because I want to be with you."

"I'm sorry, too. I said things about you and your family that I'd take back in a heartbeat if I could. My mother's addiction issues were fueled by people enabling her—people I trusted to keep me safe—which meant I had to go into the foster care system. When

McKenna showed up and took Connor, it brought back so many painful memories, and that's why I was so angry." Gage caressed her arms with his hands. "But Connor's asleep inside, and he and McKenna are both safe, and you're back. That's all that matters."

"You're being very gracious." She clasped her hands behind his neck. "Are you sure that's all you want to say?"

His smooth brow furrowed. "There is one more thing."

She knew it. Her stomach lurched. Was he going to extract himself from her embrace and tell her they didn't have a future together?

His gaze flitted to her lips for an instant. When his eyes met hers again, only approval and affection filled those gorgeous green-gold pools. "I need you, Skye. No matter what the future holds for Connor, I don't want to be apart from you anymore. I love you."

"I love you, too."

Then her eyelids fluttered, and he claimed her mouth with his. As Mr. Handsome-Hazel-Eyes deepened the kiss, she tunneled her fingers through the hair at the nape of his neck. The warmth of his touch and the comfort and safety she found in his embrace confirmed what she'd secretly known from the beginning—Gage wasn't a man who led with harsh words and intimidation. Quite the opposite. All along, he'd only used his strength to protect.

Gage sat on the Tomlinsons' couch, his arm wrapped around Skye's shoulders, and his other hand entwined with hers. He hadn't stopped holding on to her since she'd raced up the driveway and back into his life over an hour ago, and until Mrs. Tomlinson sent him home, he had no plans to let go. McKenna and Mrs. Tomlinson sat across from them, staring at him expectantly.

"Gage?" Skye squeezed his hand. "Did you hear McKenna?"

"I—I'm sorry, I didn't." He grinned at her. "Got distracted."

Her mouth curved into a knowing smile, drawing his gaze to the fullness of her lower lip. His arms ached to pull her into another embrace and re-create their reunion on the front porch, but not with her mother and cousin as an audience. He tore his gaze away and forced himself to focus on McKenna.

"I said I want you and Skye to be Connor's legal guardians."

"What?"

"Since you're together—I'm assuming that's the case, since you can't stop staring or touching each other." McKenna's eyes gleamed with tears as she offered a wobbly smile. "I want you to be his permanent guardians."

His pulse spiked. Was she serious? And how was that even possible? He and Skye weren't married or even engaged. Not that he hadn't thought about both those events happening in the very near future. He opened his mouth to respond, but the words wouldn't come. "What about Gerald and Irene?"

"I've been in touch with an attorney," Mrs. Tomlinson said. "He's preparing a response in case they sue for custody."

"Not that I have any right to be critical, but Irene was not very hands-on as a mother. Ryan told me once that she was way more interested in her hobbies than him." McKenna twisted a tissue around her fingers. "I should have told you sooner because he said that whatever happened between us, he didn't want his parents raising Connor."

The hair on the back of Gage's neck stood up. That explained why Ryan hadn't spent a lot of time talking about his parents. "When did he say that?"

"He wrote it in an email. I still have it." McKenna glanced at Mrs. Tomlinson. "At least I did one thing right."

"Don't be too hard on yourself," Mrs. Tomlinson said. "You're being very brave."

Gage's mind raced, eager to map out the facts.

"After I told him I was pregnant, he asked me to move to Florida. I said I was too afraid to move that far, especially when he spent so much time at sea, and I didn't have any support. That's when he said he could borrow money from his parents to help me move, but if they found out about the baby, he warned me they'd… be a challenge to deal with."

McKenna dabbed at her tears with the tissue. "Ryan wanted Connor to have a different childhood than he did."

Gage released a heavy sigh. Skye's thumb slid gently across the back of his hand, offering comfort.

"I know this is a big decision, but I'm not capable of taking care of Connor on my own. I—I'm scared I'll just keep hurting him."

"Oh, sweetheart." Mrs. Tomlinson pulled McKenna close. "We are going to figure this out. Together. It's getting late. Why don't you try to get some sleep?"

McKenna nodded and pushed to her feet. Her teary-eyed gaze lingered on Skye and Gage. "Please think about what I said."

"We will." Skye's eyes flitted to his, and the tenderness there filled him with love. She'd make such an amazing mother, to Connor and to any future children they had together. Warmth crawled up his neck at the image of a house full of kids. For the second time in only a few minutes, he forced himself to rein in his thoughts.

"Looks like you two have a lot to talk about. I'll help McKenna get settled in the guest room." Mrs. Tomlinson stood and followed McKenna down the hall. "Don't stay up too late."

When they were alone, Gage dipped his head and brushed his lips against Skye's. "I've been waiting almost an hour to do that."

Her soft laughter made his heart beat double time. "I thought they'd never go to bed."

While he wanted to kiss her senseless, Mrs. Tomlinson had gently hinted that he ought to go soon, and they still had so much to talk about. He straightened and put a fraction of an inch between them, just so he could think straight. And ask her the question that had been top of mind since she'd come back to Merritt's Crossing.

"Are you still going back to Denver?"

"Nope. I'll call my boss first thing tomorrow and resign."

He felt the tiniest embers of hope ignite.

"What about you? Still heading for Wyoming in the morning?"

He studied her. "Who told you?"

Eyes gleaming, she shook her head in mock disbelief. "If you're going to live in Merritt's Crossing, you'll have to accept what I'm about to tell you as absolute fact."

"Oh? What's that?"

"We all make it our business to know everyone else's business."

He nodded. "Good to know. Sounds like my kind of place."

Her eyes grew wide. "Does that mean you'll stay?"

"Only if you will."

She grinned. "I hear there's a furniture store that still has hope of surviving and a little boy who needs a mom and a dad."

"I thought motherhood wasn't part of your long game. What changed your mind?"

Reaching up to cup his cheek with her palm, she stared deeply into his eyes. "Connor. And you."

Goose bumps raced across his skin. "What do you think about McKenna's request?"

She stared at him for what seemed like an eternity. "I plan to say yes, but I need to know if you're willing to take on a family? Because Connor and I are a package deal."

Tears pricked his eyelids, but he battled them back. Reaching for her hand, he pressed a kiss to the inside of her wrist. "Nothing in the world would make me happier than to build a life with you and be Connor's dad." His voice cracked. "Marry me?"

"Yes." Her heavy-lidded gaze made warmth flare. "Now, kiss me again."

He moved within inches of her mouth, drinking her in, memorizing every curve of her face before he complied with her request.

The realization that they were planning a life together seeped into him, chasing away the guilt and regret that had plagued him for far too long. While he'd valued his time in the navy and the structure offered by the military lifestyle, it had enabled him to avoid any serious romantic relationships. While he'd once equated family and intimacy with pain and rejection, Skye gave him the courage to risk his heart again. Finding Connor and meeting the Tomlinsons taught him what a real family looked like, not only the faults but the unconditional love, too. He'd kept his word to Ryan and gained more than he ever dreamed possible.

Epilogue

One year later

Skye was glad she'd said yes.

Yes to McKenna's request to become Connor's guardian, yes to staying in Merritt's Crossing and, most of all, yes to Gage's marriage proposal.

"You look stunning." Laramie caught her gaze in the mirror hanging in the church's Sunday school classroom that they'd transformed into a makeshift dressing area as she adjusted the gauzy veil pinned carefully around Skye's elegant French twist.

"Thank you." Skye admired the long-sleeved gown with a fitted lace bodice that tapered down to her waist and then billowed out into a full satin skirt with flowers embroidered along the hemline.

She smiled at her reflection, then turned and hugged her best friend and maid of honor. "We couldn't have pulled this wedding off without your help."

"Nonsense," Laramie said. "You did most of the planning."

"I want today to be amazing. For me and for Gage."

Waiting a whole year to become Mrs. Gage Westbrook

had been challenging, and more than once they'd seriously considered eloping at the county courthouse. But since they were about to become a family of three in a most nontraditional way, having an intimate traditional ceremony and reception with their closest friends and family was important. Connor meant the world to both of them, but they'd dedicated so much time and energy to his needs.

Since the adoption was finalized and they were officially Connor's mother and father now, today was meant to be a celebration of their love as they became husband and wife.

Skye's legs trembled, and goose bumps raced down her spine. She wasn't apprehensive—just overwhelmed with joy. For a long time, she'd written off the possibility of ever wearing a gown like this. Scarcely allowed herself to dream of one day walking down the aisle toward a man like Gage.

But God, in His infinite love and grace, had healed the broken places and orchestrated something beautiful where once she'd only seen chaos and heartache.

"I've loved every minute of this hectic whirlwind that's become your life, by the way." Laramie popped open a compact and quickly powdered Skye's nose one more time. "It's been quite a year, hasn't it?"

"It has," she agreed. "Today couldn't get here soon enough."

Between Gage's long hours at Alta Vista's wind farm and her efforts to turn the furniture store into a successful business, they'd needed a year to plan the wedding and jump through all the hoops to win the custody battle waged by Ryan's parents. Thankfully, the judge had officially declared Skye and Gage Connor's parents and granted Gerald and Irene weekend visitation once every other month. They were required to come to Colorado to spend time with Connor.

Laramie checked her own reflection in the mirror one last time, smoothed her hands over the simple navy satin bridesmaid's dress with the floral lace overlay, then stepped into her sling-back heels.

A knock sounded at the door and her mother and Bethany came in, wearing dresses similar to Laramie's.

"Oh, look at you." Mom splayed her hand across her chest, eyes glistening with tears.

"No crying." Bethany fanned Mom's face with her hand. "If you start, we won't be able to stop."

"I'm so happy for you, sweetheart." Her mom gently pulled Skye into an embrace and then tenderly kissed her cheek. "You are going to make Gage very happy, and you are already an incredible mother to Connor."

"Thank you," Skye whispered, determined not to melt into a puddle of tears before she and Gage saw each other.

They picked up their bouquets, and the photographer slipped in and took more pictures. When she was finished, Laramie circled around behind Skye and lifted the train of her gown. "C'mon, you've kept your groom waiting long enough."

They moved slowly toward the door. Skye heard Connor's contagious laugh echoing out in the hallway, and she smiled. Drew said something, his voice muffled, and Connor giggled again. He'd been the star of the show last night at the rehearsal dinner. Hopefully between Drew and Jack, they'd steer him down the aisle as the ring bearer and keep him occupied during the ceremony. It was a lot to ask of a two-year-old, but she couldn't imagine not including him.

Mom was babysitting Connor for the next five days,

but once she and Gage came home from their honey-moon in Estes Park, near Rocky Mountain National Park, they'd finally be a family of three.

As the bridal party moved toward the closed double doors at the back of the sanctuary, the violinist's prelude filtered through the air.

Connor caught sight of Skye, toddled over to her in his miniature gray suit and reached for her hand. He tipped his head up and offered a smile. "Mama."

How could two little syllables make her heart soar? "Hey, pumpkin. You look handsome."

The doors opened, and Drew seated Mom in the front row. Connor wiggled uncontrollably, his chubby hand still clasping hers. While she waited for Drew to return so he and Jack could both walk her down the aisle and into her future with the man she loved, she stared at Connor in amazement.

It was incredible how one little guy had burst into her life, brought Gage to Merritt's Crossing and forged an unbreakable bond.

* * * * *

Dear Reader,

Have you ever felt absolutely convinced you were on the right path, but your current reality doesn't look anything like you'd anticipated? When I set out to write *Their Baby Blessing*, I couldn't pinpoint the deeper theme of the story. As I brainstormed the hero and heroine, it became apparent that Skye was going to be a fiercely independent character, with aspirations and expectations for her life, yet circumstances would arise that challenged her plans. Then about halfway through the first draft, I realized aspects of Skye's struggle with wanting to do her own thing and doubting God's faithfulness mirrored my real-life struggles and doubts.

It's a challenge, isn't it? Sometimes life doesn't look like we thought it would, and we misinterpret our circumstances as our opportunity to step in and take control. Thankfully, control is just an illusion and God is always faithful, even when we wrestle with doubt. He often has plans that far exceed our wildest expectations, including blessings we never envisioned receiving. I hope this is the message you take with you long after you finish reading Gage, Skye and Connor's story.

Thank you for reading this book. I love hearing from readers, and you can find me on Facebook, Twitter, Instagram and at heidimccahan.com. All subscribers to my e-newsletter receive a free novella that isn't available anywhere else. By the way, if you enjoyed *Their Baby Blessing* and would post an honest review online, I'd be grateful.

Sincerely,
Heidi McCahan

Yasmin shifted on the glider, set it rocking with one foot and tucked the other foot up under her. The air was cooling now, a slight breeze bringing the fragrance of oleander flowers. It seemed only natural for Liam to shuffle closer on the glider. To let his arm curve around her shoulders.

Yasmin's breath whooshed out of her. Talking with Liam about her brother had made her feel vulnerable, but also relieved. Less alone. She remembered when she could share anything with Liam and he would always have her back. Such a wonderful feeling, especially after her brother had stopped being able to be that rock and that support to her.

Now Liam turned to meet her gaze head-on. His hand rose to brush back a curl that had escaped her ponytail. "I like your hairstyle," he said unexpectedly, his voice a tone deeper than usual. "Reminds me of the old days, when we were in school."

"In other words, I look like a kid?" Her words came out breathy, and she couldn't take her eyes off him.

Slowly, Liam shook his head. "Oh, no, Yasmin. You don't look like a kid at all." His eyes flickered down to her mouth, then back to her eyes.

Yasmin's heart fluttered like a terrified bird. Her stomach, her chest, all that was inside her felt squeezed by warm hands, melting.

How she wanted this. This opportunity to talk to Liam in a low, intimate voice. To feel that sense of promise, that there was something happy and bright in their future together.

She tried to grasp on to the reasons why this couldn't happen. How she didn't dare to have children, because the risk of them developing a mental illness was so high. Not only because of Josiah, although that was the main thing, of course. But also because of her mother's issues.

As if all of that wasn't enough, Yasmin knew she wasn't past the safe age herself. What if she got into a relationship and then started having delusions and hearing voices?

It was hard enough taking care of her brother, her blood relative. She owed him and bore the burden gladly. But she couldn't expect a romantic partner to do the same for her, wouldn't want someone to.

Wouldn't want Liam to.

If she let things go where they were headed right now, if she let him kiss her, she wasn't sure she would have the strength to push him away again. Doing it once had nearly killed her. Maybe she could be strong enough, but only if she put an end to this before getting closer. "I think we should go."

His head tilted to one side, his eyes steady on her. "Do you really think so?"

She hesitated, clung for just a moment to the possibility of not being the responsible one, the caretaker, the one who took charge of things and tried to make everything work out. She could let herself do what she wanted to do every now and then, couldn't she? She could be spontaneous, go with her emotions, her heart.

But no. Her duty was clear. Her life was about taking care of her family, not about indulging in something pleasurable for now, but ultimately dangerous to someone she cared about. Liam was too good of a man, had suffered too many of life's blows already, to be shackled with Yasmin's issues. "Yes," she said firmly. "I really think so."

Don't miss Lee Tobin McClain's
Low Country Dreams, *available June 2019*
wherever Harlequin® books and ebooks are sold.

www.Harlequin.com

PHLTMEXP0619

Looking for inspiration in tales
of hope, faith and heartfelt romance?

Check out **Love Inspired**® and
Love Inspired® **Suspense** books!

New books available every month!

CONNECT WITH US AT:

Facebook.com/groups/HarlequinConnection

 Facebook.com/HarlequinBooks

Twitter.com/HarlequinBooks

Instagram.com/HarlequinBooks

Pinterest.com/HarlequinBooks

ReaderService.com